Unstable

Hooked #4

Charity Parkerson

--Warning: This book is intended for readers over the age of 18.

Author Note

I've never shied away from writing about controversial topics and non-traditional relationships because everyone is different and deserving of a happy-ever-after.

With that said, in this case, I've decided to add this note as a trigger warning. This book involves some tragic topics, such as past child abuse. It may not be an easy read. It wasn't easy to write, but this is Jimmy and Eli's story. They deserve happiness too.

Introduction

"A bottle of liquor a day keeps the demons at bay."

After a childhood so horrific a book was published about it, Jimmy understandably didn't become the most well-adjusted adult. He's made it his business to blend into the background while drinking himself into an early grave. That is, until he pulls a homeless teen from the dumpster.

Living on the streets hasn't been easy for Eli. Anything is better than the life he left behind. Strangers haven't always had the best of intentions when they claim they want to help. Jimmy is different. That doesn't mean Eli won't rob him blind and disappear into the night.

When Eli returns, older and prepared to repay his debt, he never expects to give up more than his savings to the sexy bar owner. Sometimes, it takes two people who've seen hell to create heaven. Unfortunately, they'll have to face their demons if they hope to make it work between them.

Chapter 1

Unstable. That was what Eli's dad had called him before he'd kicked him out. In all his teenage rage, he'd puffed out his chest, flipped the old man a bird, and owned that shit. Yeah. He was a little off. Maybe he did shit even he couldn't explain, but didn't most teenagers? That was two years ago. Now, at seventeen, Eli didn't feel the same rage. Oh, he was still pissed as hell, but for different reasons. Back then, he'd been all teenage angst and thinking the world owed him more. Now, he recognized how hard shit really was. He realized what the world really owed him was better parents.

Fuck it. He didn't need anyone. Living

in the streets fucking sucked. He couldn't lie. It'd be nice to sleep in a real bed and get a hot shower on the regular. But not if it meant getting punched around. This was better. His stomach growled, making a liar out of him. Tonight would be a cold one. Eli hated the thought of going hungry and freezing. One was bad enough on its own without adding the other.

The dumpster behind Jimmy's Bar usually got picked up by the city on Tuesdays. For some reason, they were a day behind. Maybe it was a holiday? Eli hadn't been sure of the date in a long time. He wasn't one to look too closely at a blessing. After dragging a crate closer, Eli climbed on and dug in. All he needed was a little bit of liquor to get him through the cold night—make him not care about his aching and empty stomach. He'd yet to find an alcohol that tasted good, but Eli wasn't worried about that. It was the oblivion he sought. He hated himself a little for seeking its warmth. When it was well below freezing, Eli had to let some morals go.

A squeal—like metal scraping metal—was the only warning Eli got before the back door to Jimmy's swung open, spilling light onto the darkened pavement. A large figure blocked out the light. Without thought, Eli dove head first into the smelly pile of garbage. It wasn't a soft or quiet landing. Something sharp scraped his arm and stabbed him in the back. Right away, he knew he hadn't been quick enough. A loud yell rent the air. The clanging of bottles banging against each other beneath him drowned out the man's words. Eli tried shifting his weight, hoping to spring from the dumpster. Before he got his bearings, a face appeared above him.

Blond hair surrounded the man's face—like a halo, hiding his features from sight. His shoulders were massive, blocking out the sky. Eli's breaths came out in bursts, sounding loud even to his ears. His heart beat too fast to deliver oxygen to Eli's starved brain. He couldn't think of a way to escape.

"Damn, kid. What are you doing? Don't you know homeless guys puke in that fucking dumpster? Get the fuck out of there." Without waiting for Eli to do as told, the dude plucked him out of the dumpster using one arm. Eli's eyes widened. One second, he'd been on his back in the trash. The next, the world whirled past him until he was upright and on his feet.

"Holy shit." That was all he had. The guy's arms were huge. Deep ridges and hard mounds made up some impressive muscles. It was on the tip of his tongue to ask if he worked out, but even Eli recognized how stupid that would be. "That was incredible. I bet you can lift five hundred pounds."

The stranger snorted. "You can't weigh more than eighty-five soaking wet. That's hardly five hundred."

"Well, I *am* one of those homeless freaks who pukes in trashcans, so what did you expect?"

While still holding Eli by the collar, the dude leaned closer and sniffed. "Yeah, I figured that by the smell of you."

Eli's throat swelled unexpectedly. He couldn't explain why he cared what this stranger thought. "Nobody's forcing you to endure my company. I'm out of here." He tried taking a step away. The dude held tight to his shirt, ensuring Eli went nowhere.

"Look, kid, I'm the worst sort of asshole, but I'm not about to let some thirteen-year-old go wandering off in the middle of the night. It's supposed to drop to below twenty degrees. Where are your parents?"

Eli's mouth fell open. He tried to decide which part he was most offended by. For real, he didn't know where to start first. "I'm not thirteen. For your information, I'm seventeen, and I don't have any fucking parents. If I want to freeze my balls off, that's my business. Shove off." He tried prying loose. The ease with which the man held on to Eli was not only ridiculous but maddening. Eli may as well have been a fly for all the notice the guy paid his efforts.

With a deep sigh, the stranger headed for the back door of the bar, dragging Eli along. "Come on, kid. I can't leave you out

11

here."

Panic rose in Eli's chest. He didn't know this guy. He could be a serial killer or worse, he could call someone who'd take him back to his parents. Eli dragged his feet, trying to slow him down. "No way, dude. Let go. I've heard about people like you. I ain't sucking no dick to get warm."

A low rumble of laughter drifted through the air. Chill bumps rose on Eli's skin that had nothing to do with the cold. Words failed him. His gaze locked on the man's wide shoulders. He wasn't wearing a jacket. Funny, Eli hadn't noticed before now. He wasn't even shivering. Eli's mouth went dry. He licked his lips. They stung, reminding him how chapped they were. After throwing open the back door, the man waved Eli inside. Eli refused to budge.

"I'm not allowed inside a bar."

The man rolled his eyes. Eli couldn't look away. They were blue. He'd known they were light in coloration, but it had been hard to tell an exact color in the dark. With the light spilling from inside the bar and casting a glow around him, Eli could see them now. They were the same color as the sky in the summertime.

"No doubt you do a lot of things you're not allowed to do. I won't tell if you don't."

Eli licked his lips again and winced. Why couldn't he remember to stop doing that? The man's gaze dropped to Eli's mouth. He knew the dude didn't mean anything by it. Eli was certain they looked as bad as they felt. But with the man's gaze lingering on his mouth, Eli's already too small jeans tightened. His gaze snapped back to the stranger's when he realized what he'd been doing.

"Look, I'm Jimmy," the stranger said,

holding his hand out for Eli to shake, as if he was the dude's equal and not covered in God knows what.

Eli accepted, but he tried making it quick. For some reason he couldn't explain, he didn't want to dirty Jimmy with his touch. "Eli."

Jimmy nodded. "This is my place. No one will bother you here, especially me. I can't leave you out in the cold." Eli didn't react. He didn't know what to say. The man definitely could leave him out in the cold. His parents had. What did it matter if Jimmy did? Thankfully, Jimmy didn't seem to need any words from Eli to continue. "Just come in and warm up. Get some food in your stomach and whatnot. If you don't want to stay the night, I can't keep you here, but give it an hour. Okay?"

His feet moved before Eli realized he'd decided to accept. "Just an hour," Eli agreed. His gaze refused to budge from Jimmy's face as he passed. He wasn't scared. Not really. There was an uneasy stirring in Eli's gut, but it wasn't fear. He wasn't sure what it was. Warmth engulfed him as he stepped over the threshold. Eli cast a look around. There was a couch and a desk to his left. To his right, he spotted the darkened bar through an open doorway. They'd closed hours earlier. Eli would know. He'd been waiting for his chance to raid the dumpster.

"There's nothing hot in the kitchen, but I can make you a sandwich."

Eli jumped as Jimmy spoke at his back. Okay, so there was a sliver of fear hiding away in his heart. No one was ever nice to him without wanting something in return. None of those men looked like Jimmy. At his reaction, Jimmy backed up a step. Eli's hackles went up. He wasn't a pussy.

"You don't have to do that. I'm used to going without."

Jimmy ignored him. He motioned toward a closed door behind the desk. "There's a bathroom through that door. If you want, you can take a shower. There's also some clean uniforms in the closet," he added, pointing toward a door near the couch. "You should be able to find something in your size. Get cleaned up. I'll see what food I can scrounge together." Without waiting for him to argue, Jimmy left Eli alone with his mouth hanging open. No one had ever offered him so much.

The thought of a hot shower got him moving faster than anything had in a long time. He needed to be quick. After digging through the closet and finding some clothes he thought might fit and grabbing a towel, he rushed inside the bathroom. It was tiny and perfect as far as Eli was concerned. There was nothing more than a sink, toilet, and shower. More importantly, there was a lock. Eli made sure it was set before turning on the water as hot as it would go. Steam filled the small space as Eli stepped beneath the deluge. It scalded his skin. Eli didn't flinch. Hot meant clean. He wanted to be red and squeaky. He grabbed the shampoo and popped the lid. Some tropical fruity smell assailed his nostrils. He scrubbed his hair three times before he felt satisfied with the results.

After washing every inch of his skin until it felt raw, Eli stood beneath the stream of water until it ran cold. He couldn't convince himself to put the nasty underwear back on. Commando it was. Clean clothes felt amazing against his skin. They smelled good too. He couldn't stop sniffing himself. He toweled off the mirror and stared at his reflection. Sometimes, Eli barely recognized himself any longer. Most people got bigger as they got older. Malnutrition had killed all hope for Eli. He'd grown taller, but every bone stood out. His face reminded him of a skeleton's. Dark circles shadowed his eyes, making the green stand out that much brighter. He felt a thousand years old.

His stomach growled, reminding him of Jimmy's promise of food. He spent a moment scratching at the doorknob, trying to figure out the lock in his rush. After throwing open the door wide, he slowed his pace, refusing to show how starved he was. A plate full of sandwiches, a bag of chips, and a two-liter of soda sat on the desk waiting. Eli had to force himself not to run. Jimmy was nowhere to be seen. The freedom of no witnesses had Eli rushing across the room.

He shoved half a sandwich in his mouth, nearly choking himself in the process. Oxygen became secondary to the emptiness gnawing at his gut. He'd gotten good at ignoring the hunger pains. With real food within his grasp, the cramps hit like never before. Jimmy didn't reappear until Eli had demolished half the food and most of the drink. Heat flooded Eli's cheeks when Jimmy cast a glance at the plate. The man's expression gave nothing away, freeing Eli from his embarrassment. Jimmy nodded toward the bundle of linens in his arms.

"I brought you a pillow and blanket. You can crash on the couch tonight. Tomorrow, I don't know."

Eli's hunger fled. The food sitting on

his stomach felt like a lead weight. "Where will you be sleeping?"

Jimmy snorted. "I don't go for kids, if that's what you're getting at."

Something akin to disappointment washed over Eli. He shook his head. "That's not what I meant." He swiped his sweating palms on his borrowed pants. "I guess you've got a home or something."

"Something," Jimmy agreed. "You'll be safe here. There's an alarm system. I'll set it when I leave." He held Eli's stare. "Don't get into my liquor or I will beat your ass."

The thought hadn't crossed his mind. "Okay."

Jimmy nodded, as if willing to accept Eli at his word. Eli's eyes burned. No one had ever taken him on his word alone before.

"You good for the night?"

Eli nodded, incapable of speech. Jimmy crossed the room. His arms encircled Eli. Eli sat—frozen. It wasn't a hug. Honestly, Eli didn't know what the fuck was happening. Jimmy tugged at the collar of Eli's shirt. The man's scent engulfed him along with his heat. Eli's eyes fell closed. He smelled like wintergreen gum. No one ever touched him. He didn't know how to react. His fingers curled into a ball as he fought against the urge to reach for Jimmy. There was an odd heat in his gut.

Jimmy pulled away and flashed a small white tag at him. "You forgot to take the tag off." He tossed it in the trash while Eli sat incapable of taking a full breath. This man did something to Eli's mind. He wasn't sure he liked it.

"Why are you being nice to me?" Eli

couldn't stop the question. People weren't nice for no reason, especially to him.

"I'll see you in the morning," Jimmy said, ignoring his question. "Don't open this door for anyone after I lock up. There's a lot of weirdos out there," Jimmy said, heading for the back door.

"Jimmy," Eli called before he could get away.

After setting the alarm and opening the door, Jimmy finally turned his way with his eyebrows raised in question. "Yeah?"

"Thank you." Eli had nothing else to offer the man who'd done so much for him.

Jimmy's mouth lifted in one corner in a half smirk before he winked. The odd sensation in Eli's stomach increased. Maybe he was getting sick?

"See you in the morning, Eli."

Eli swallowed past the lump in his throat. "See ya."

When the door closed, shutting him away alone, the night slammed down on Eli's shoulders. He wasn't used to sleeping indoors. He felt like he was suffocating. For a moment, he eyed the pillow and blanket. The old couch they sat upon was brown and looked as if it had seen a night or two of someone crashing on it. No doubt, it was broken in and comfortable as hell. It would definitely be the most satisfying night of sleep he'd had in ages. Instead of testing the theory, Eli walked the perimeter of the bar, checking out the rest of the building. He made sure to steer clear of the window, in case the cops drove by and thought he was robbing the place.

Bottles of liquor in every size and color lined the walls behind the bar. A small

23

glass cooler containing non-alcoholic beverages cast a soft glow on the room, lighting the path. The wooden bar gleamed and a single cash register sat quietly at the end. Against his will, Eli moved closer. He was more curious than anything. Surely Jimmy hadn't locked him inside with a stocked and unlocked register. Trusting him with the liquor was one thing. How much could he drink or take off with on foot? Money was something different. It was light, portable, and could change his life.

He eyed the buttons of the unfamiliar device. It had obviously been designed for any idiot's use. A huge green "open" button screamed Eli's name. He chewed his bottom lip. A peek wouldn't hurt. He could check inside, and then he'd know exactly how insane Jimmy was. Eli punched the button, half-expecting alarms to sound and Jimmy to jump out from his hiding spot. The drawer slid open almost silently. Silver and copper coins stared up at him from the coin tray. Eli considered slamming it closed. No one ever needed to know about his moment of weakness. His fingertips skimmed the edge. Instead of sliding it closed, Eli tugged, pulling it the rest of the way open.

Stacks of ones, fives, tens, and twenties filled each slot. The ends curled, taunting Eli to count each one. His bottom lip stung, once again reminding him how chapped his lips had become. Tomorrow night, he'd be back out on his ass in the cold. Last winter, his lips had cracked and bled. Eli had thought they'd never heal. This year would be the same. A horrible idea sneaked its way inside Eli's brain. He could borrow a few bucks—just enough to get by. His eighteenth birthday was in two weeks or so. He'd be free from the fear of being forced back home. For once, he could start a real search for a job. A life. The comfy brown couch called his name from the other room. Tonight was only one night, he reminded himself. There would be lots of cold tomorrows.

He cast a desperate look around the room, searching for answers. Moral dilemmas were new to him. This was a big one. Jimmy was nice. If Eli took this money, he might not choose to be nice ever again. Eli would ruin something untainted. His gaze landed on a small red light in the upper corner of the room. Horror chilled Eli's blood as realization dawned. It was a camera. No matter what Eli decided, Jimmy would see this footage and know Eli for the scum he was. The instant the man had left Eli alone, he'd gone straight for the cash register. He'd already ruined Jimmy's act of kindness.

In a rush, he grabbed the stacks of bills, leaving nothing behind. He checked beneath the drawer, finding a couple hundred-dollar bills. Leaving the register open wide, Eli headed for the back. First, he found a pen and paper, and scratched out a quick I-owe-you to Jimmy before going on a clothing hunt. A thick down jacket hung on a rack by the door. Eli crammed his arms inside. He found clean socks in Jimmy's desk—of all places—and a pair of gloves in a box marked as lost and found.

As he headed for the back door, Eli cast a quick glance around the room. He didn't want to miss anything, since he was already all in. His gaze landed on the blanket on the couch. He grabbed it too for good measure. Cold air blasted Eli in the face as he opened the back door. He almost reconsidered. It wasn't too late. He could put everything back where he'd found it. Possibly, Jimmy might never look at that surveillance footage. The blaring of the security alarm got Eli moving. He'd forgotten that part. Without looking back, he took off running into the night—just as he'd done the night he'd left home.

Chapter 2

Three years later...

No good bastard. That's what Jace had called him before attempting to knee him in the balls. In truth, Jimmy was shocked Jace had hung around as long as he had. Every filthy name the man had tossed in Jimmy's face was the truth. He couldn't blame Jace for breaking things off between them. That didn't mean Jimmy had stay sober over it. Too bad a liter of Jack and a fifth of Crown did nothing to squelch his headache. The pounding behind his eyes felt closer to a stroke and warned of a monster hangover. All the more reason not to sober up and grab a six-pack.

There was a banging coming from somewhere. At first, Jimmy thought the pounding in his head had moved to his ears before his gaze landed on the back door. After pushing to his feet, Jimmy stumbled for the door. If there was a God in Heaven, it wouldn't be Jace on the other side. The last thing he needed was another black mark against him in Jace's book of hate. In spite of his hope, Jimmy had no clue who else would bang down the back door of his bar at three in the morning.

He tried smoothing out the wrinkles in his shirt. Giving up, he ran his fingers through his hair, hoping it wasn't too bad. That was a lost cause. Fuck it. Jace hated him too much to care. He pushed the door open and froze. In his current state, it didn't take much to lock down his brain. Finding a stranger on his stoop proved too much for the liquor-soaked organ living inside his head.

"Hey, Jimmy."

The stranger knew his name. "Um.

Hey."

As if he found Jimmy's confusion humorous, the man smiled. "May I come in?"

Jimmy chewed on the inside of his cheek, mulling things over. The dude didn't look dangerous or crazy, but neither did Jimmy, and he was both. He took a step back. Jimmy eyed the man as he passed. He was small—maybe only five-eight. His hair was a dark, choppy mess, as if he didn't get it cut or comb it often. Considering the package and Jimmy's lack of memory, he could only assume they'd slept together.

He closed the door. The man turned. He inspected the stranger's features in the light. He was young—way too young for Jimmy's tastes. His mind whirled again. No way had they slept together.

"I'd offer you a beer, but I get the feeling you're not legal."

The man's smile grew. "You have no idea who I am, do you?"

Jimmy shrugged. "If you're about to claim you're my kid or some shit, you can save it. Not only do I not chase women, I never have."

His nighttime visitor's expression transformed. The smile fell. Something unnamed flashed in his eyes, disappearing before Jimmy could grasp it. "Um." The man shifted from foot to foot, looking more uncomfortable by the moment. "I have to admit, I wasn't expecting you not to remember. You took me in about three years ago."

Memories flooded Jimmy's brain. This was the homeless kid? "Eli?"

He nodded.

A growl rose in Jimmy's throat. "I should toss your ass in the street. You're a brave little fucker, showing your face around here after stealing a solid grand from me."

Eli didn't back down. It was a point in his favor. "That's why I'm here."

Jimmy's eyebrows hit his hairline at the claim. "What? Was a grand not enough? Are you back for more?"

The kid's expression never wavered. "No."

His head spun. "Fuck. I'm too tired to care," Jimmy said, moving for the couch. In an odd way, he was glad to see Eli. More times than he could count, Jimmy had thought of the skinny homeless kid he'd pulled out of the trash and wondered if he was okay. Now, here he was—clean and healthy looking.

After dropping down on one end of the couch, he motioned Eli toward the other. "If you're not here to steal more money from me, why are you here?" Jimmy asked as Eli crossed the room and sat.

"I've been working at Hollow Edge. It's a clothing store in the mall," Eli explained instead of answering. "It's thanks to the money I stole from you, actually."

Jimmy blinked at him in confusion. "Okay."

Undeterred by the sarcasm dripping from Jimmy's voice, Eli continued. "No one had ever been nice to me before you," Eli said, sounding sad.

Jimmy was—for the most part—unmoved. "So you repaid me by stealing from me. Makes sense. That's pretty par for the course in my life. Go on."

Eli eyed him in silence for a moment

before digging an envelope out of his back pocket and holding it out to Jimmy. "It's taken me three years of saving a little at a time, but here's the money I took."

Jimmy stared at the worn-looking envelope. He couldn't bring himself to reach for it. When he didn't take it, Eli set it on the cushion between them.

"I'm sorry it took me so long. Between paying the rent on my room, buying food, and all that, it's been a struggle." He held Jimmy's gaze without blinking. "But even if it had taken me a hundred years, I'd always planned to pay you back."

Jimmy swallowed past his rapidly drying throat. He was used to dealing with the dregs of the universe. This was different. He tried speaking but only managed one word. "Why?"

Eli's face hardened. "I'm no thief."

"No," Jimmy said, realizing Eli misunderstood. "Why did you steal from me in the first place? If you'd asked, I would've given you the money." The funny thing was—Jimmy meant it. When he'd pulled the scraggly kid from the trash, he'd been... moved. He couldn't explain it, but Jimmy knew he would've helped Eli if the boy had asked.

Eli looked away. His cheeks reddened. Jimmy regretted the question. Before he could tell Eli not to answer, Eli opened his mouth and wiped Jimmy's mind. "I'd never had anyone as sexy as you do a damn thing for me. Especially not for free." Jimmy spent a moment wondering who he should kill, but Eli kept talking. "I took the money and rented a room at the Pay-by-Week over on 8th. Then I got a pre-paid phone and some clothes before heading out to pepper the town with applications.

It was hard," Eli said, as if admitting a dirty secret. "A grand doesn't go far, even when you're like me and used to having nothing at all." He held Jimmy's gaze. "Luckily, Hollow Edge called and offered me a job before I ran through all the money. I've limped by, but I always intended to pay you back."

Jimmy shifted to his feet and headed for the door. He held it open for Eli. "I don't want it."

Eli eyed the open doorway but didn't budge.

Jimmy massaged the ache at his temples that hadn't ebbed with Eli's arrival. "Look, kid."

"I'm twenty."

"And I'm thirty-two," Jimmy shot back. "So, *kid*, I'm glad I was able to help you out. As I said earlier, I would've given you the money if you'd asked. No harm. No foul. Take your savings and hang on to it for a rainy day. Now, if you don't mind, I was in the middle of drinking myself into an early grave when you arrived. I'd like to get back to it."

Still, Eli didn't budge. "Every day is a rainy day for me. I get the feeling every day is a new opportunity to drink yourself into an early grave for you. So, if you don't mind, I'd like to stay and convince you to keep the money."

Jimmy shook his head. "I'm not keeping that money."

"Then I'm not leaving," Eli shot back, looking damnably calm for someone who was about to go ass over teakettle into the street.

Jimmy slammed the door shut. "Suit yourself," he growled as he headed for the six-pack he'd forgotten on the desk. He popped one open and chugged half before facing Eli again. "Why is this so important to you? If someone told me I didn't owe them shit, I wouldn't owe them shit."

"I need to know we're square."

Jimmy's brows drew together. "Why?" He took a step in Eli's direction. The room spun. Eli shot to his feet, steadying Jimmy before he hit the floor. Eli's face was inches from Jimmy's. He had a smattering of freckles across the bridge of his nose. He looked young. Innocent. His eyes were a shade of light green Jimmy had never seen before. Not only were they amazing, they were also focused on Jimmy's mouth. It only seemed fair for Jimmy to drop his gaze to Eli's lips. The kid was pretty. "Thanks," Jimmy muttered, pulling out of Eli's hold. "Didn't think I'd gotten that far into my cups yet. Hopefully, this next beer will put me over the edge." He took a step back, intent on grabbing another drink. Eli took a step forward, refusing to allow Jimmy to put space between them.

"Don't you think you've had enough?"

No one had challenged him in a long time. His blood sang. He popped the tab on another beer, daring Eli with his gaze to say something else. Before he could lift the can to his lips, Eli snagged the can and held it behind his back. If Jimmy had been sober, there was no way Eli would've pulled off taking away his alcohol. In his drunken state, Jimmy made a huge mistake. He went after it. After closing the gap between them, he reached behind Eli's back, intent on reclaiming his drink. The instant their bodies collided, Jimmy's flared to life in a way it hadn't in years. Guilt snaked in. This child didn't need a grown man pawing at him. He was such an ass. The smell of burning rubber from Jace's tires, as he'd raced from Jimmy's life, hadn't yet dissipated. Jimmy's body was already on fire from someone else's touch—like it had never been for Jace.

"I'm with someone." Before the words finished leaving his lips, Jimmy wanted them back. What an obnoxious, egomaniacally ass he was to assume Eli's body had reacted the same as his.

Eli didn't pull from his hold. "What's his name?"

"Jace."

"Sounds sweet."

At the observation, Jimmy took a step back, giving up on his drink. "I guess I've had enough after all."

Eli set the beer on the desk. His expression sat on Jimmy's chest, making it hard for him to breathe. He imagined the man would look the same if Jimmy punched him.

"Sorry. You're a grown man. I shouldn't have…" He ran his hand through his dark hair, leaving it standing on end. He squared his shoulders and met Jimmy's stare. "Thank you for everything you did for me. I'll leave you—"

Jimmy kissed him. God help him. He couldn't resist. There was this itch beneath his skin. He couldn't let this man get away without one taste. If Jimmy never saw Eli again, he'd wonder for the rest of his life. The reaction he'd experienced when their bodies touched had nothing on their lips meeting. Air rushed from Jimmy's lungs and didn't reappear. It was the most innocent kiss Jimmy had ever experienced, and still, it was also the hottest. Neither of them sought to deepen the kiss. Their tongues didn't meet. Jimmy stood, hands at his sides, with Eli's bottom lip held between his. He'd never been more afraid of tainting someone in his life.

The back door flew open. The trance holding Jimmy enthralled slowly slipped away at the sight of Jace filling the doorway. Horror overcame him. Jace stood with a stack of clothes in his arms, staring at Jimmy with a level of hatred he'd never seen the man show. His normally sweet brown eyes flashed with anger as he took in the situation.

"Wow. Seducing a teenager in the back room of a bar—classy. I shouldn't be surprised." He tossed the clothes in Jimmy's direction. "I found these while cleaning out my car. They're yours." His gaze slid Eli's way. Jimmy fought the urge to place his body between the two men. Eli wasn't the one at fault here. "He'll destroy your life," Jace promised before turning away and leaving the back door standing open. Jimmy blinked at the open doorway, unsure of what to do. Jace had broken up with him. He didn't owe the man anything. The knowledge didn't stop him from feeling like the biggest dick on the planet. Jimmy's gaze slid Eli's way. His face was free of all emotion, but his eyes burned.

His gaze collided with Jimmy's. "Jace?"

Jimmy nodded.

Eli's gaze hit the ceiling and he blew out a long breath. "I am such a loser." Without a backward glance or giving Jimmy time to think of a response, Eli stepped around Jimmy and escaped out the open door. Jimmy cast a desperate glance around the room, trying to decide what had just happened. His gaze landed on a worn-looking envelope on the couch.

"Fuck." The kid had left the money.

*

Eli kept an eye on two teenage boys who looked to be around fourteen. He had a bad feeling they were talking each other into pocketing some merchandise. They glanced his way and caught him watching them. Both boys took off out the door. An inner sigh rang through Eli's head. Had he ever been that young? In all honesty, Eli didn't think he'd ever been young—period. Tonight, he felt especially old. Working at Hollow Edge was the best his life would ever be. He couldn't afford to do more. Hell, he couldn't even afford dinner. The thought had him glancing at the clock on his register.

"It's time for my lunch break," Eli said, letting his co-worker, Alisha, know he was heading out before grabbing his coat from underneath the register. They were too dead tonight for anyone to make a fuss.

"Good. I'm right on time."

Eli froze at the familiar voice. Alisha's eyes widened as her gaze slid over Eli's shoulder. He knew exactly what she was seeing—over six feet of delicious god. The long blond hair. The blue eyes. Eli's stomach growled. The solid muscles. He swallowed past the lust burning in his throat and turned. Jimmy looked every bit as sexy as Eli pictured every night when he closed his eyes.

"Don't you have a bar to run?"

"It has a good manager," Jimmy said. His gaze slipped down Eli's body as he made the claim. Eli stood still for the inspection, wishing he didn't feel quite so lacking while standing next to Jimmy.

"How long do you get for dinner?" Jimmy asked, meeting Eli's gaze once more.

Eli licked his lips. There was no escape. "Thirty minutes."

"Guess we'd better hurry, then."

Without thought, he stepped around the register, moving closer to Jimmy. His feet didn't care that his brain was scared shitless. They were headed where his body wanted to be—with his sexy savior.

"How did you know where to find me?"

A dark-sounding chuckle rumbled from Jimmy's chest at Eli's question. "You told me where you work last night. I took a chance you'd be here."

"I'm surprised you remember anything from last night," Eli admitted as he fell into step beside Jimmy. He had no idea where they were headed nor did he care. They could circle the mall all night. Jimmy could lead him into hell. It didn't matter at all.

"Never in my life have I been so drunk I don't remember anything." He cast a sideways look at Eli. "Don't ever believe a man if he claims different."

"What about tonight?"

"What about it?" Jimmy asked, sounding only mildly curious.

"Are you sober now?"

"Ish," Jimmy answered, heading for the food court. "What are you in the mood for?"

Such a loaded question coming from such a sexy man, it hurt Eli's chest. "It doesn't matter. I can't afford to eat." Damn, he hated saying those words. His pride stung, but he couldn't make money appear that didn't exist.

"Don't think I asked you about money. I asked what you're in the mood for."

His ego wouldn't withstand the blow. "I'm not hungry."

The low and long sigh escaping Jimmy had Eli biting back a chuckle. "How about we sit in my truck instead? I think we need to talk."

Eli was so damn glad not to be on the spot over the food, he was willing to discuss whatever Jimmy wanted, even that kiss gone wrong. Not to mention, sitting alone with this man in the dark sounded like freaking heaven to him. "Sure."

Changing directions, Jimmy headed for the parking lot. Eli had a hard time keeping up with the man's long stride. Lack of food and sleep wasn't helping matters. When he reached the passenger side of a newer model F150, Jimmy waited for Eli to catch up before opening the door and motioning Eli inside.

It seemed there should've been a hint of fear inside Eli. Just as the night they'd met, Eli allowed Jimmy to lure him into being alone with barely a single qualm. He climbed inside without argument. Jimmy closed the door behind him before circling the truck and crawling in behind the wheel. Logically, Eli knew Jimmy could fire the vehicle to life and take him anywhere. A trill of excitement ran through him at the thought. He'd never been anywhere before. This town was his home. Most likely, he'd never leave it. Reality crashed down on Eli's shoulders, bringing with it a wave of sadness. He'd never be anything—go anywhere.

Jimmy slid closer. Eli didn't move. A

tiny voice inside Eli's brain screamed for the man to kiss him—the way he'd done the night before. Their faces were only inches apart. Eli could close the distance between them, making the first move. Cowardice held him in check. Alcohol had fueled Jimmy's kiss last night. No doubt, sober, the man wouldn't dream of touching Eli. Still, he couldn't tear his gaze away from Jimmy's face. The man's features were cut to perfection. There was a dimple in his chin. Eli realized he'd never seen Jimmy smile—not really. Not enough to know if there were dimples in his cheeks as well.

"Do you ever smile?" The question slipped from Eli without his permission. Jimmy reached behind Eli's seat and grabbed a cooler.

He set it between them. "I'll smile if you share this food with me."

Eli eyed the contents of the ice chest as Jimmy popped it open. It was the same basic meal Jimmy fed him three years ago. It looked like a feast.

"See," Jimmy continued. "I figured you wouldn't let me buy you dinner, but I hoped you'd at least share a sandwich with me."

Eli's gaze shifted from the food to Jimmy's hopeful expression. "And you'll smile if I agree?"

Jimmy nodded. It was a solemn gesture. Eli took him at his word. He reached inside the cooler and grabbed a ham and cheese. His stomach growled. Jimmy smiled at the sound. Everything inside Eli froze at the sight. Even his lungs refused to work. He did have dimples. Amazing dimples that transformed his entire face, making him seem younger. They stole every thought from Eli's head, including his embarrassment over his growling stomach.

"You're beautiful."

Jimmy's smile fell. "I'm rotten, Eli. All the way to my core. Don't ever forget it, okay?"

Eli refused to agree.

Jimmy sighed. "Eat your sandwich. The clock is ticking on your lunch break and we still need to talk." Eli took a bite because Jimmy said to. Jimmy nodded as if satisfied Eli would do as told. "I shouldn't have kissed you last night."

The food turned to ash in Eli's mouth. He swallowed, hoping it would stay down. He knew Jimmy was right and that didn't make things better. "I know you're with someone."

Jimmy shook his head. "That's not it.

You're too young for someone as jaded as I am."

A low laugh escaped Eli. An unfamiliar sensation tugged at the corners of his mouth. "That's hilarious."

Jimmy's gaze dropped to his mouth. Eli swiped at his lips, wondering if he had food covering his face. Finding nothing, he dropped his hand. Jimmy's gaze didn't budge.

"Why is that funny?"

Eli shrugged, deciding to ignore the way Jimmy was looking at him. "My dad used to beat me almost every day until I tried stabbing him and he kicked me out at fifteen. Living on the streets wasn't better, in case you were wondering. I'm pretty sure I have the market cornered on being jaded."

"There are a lot of shitty men in the

world, fighting demons they can't control," Jimmy said, still staring at Eli's mouth.

"Even you?" Eli shot back before he could stop himself, since Jimmy had claimed he was rotten to the core.

Jimmy's gaze lifted, meeting Eli's. "Especially me." Instead of elaborating, Jimmy reached into the ice chest and grabbed a sandwich. After taking a bite, he rooted around until he found two drinks. He passed one Eli's way. They ate in silence. Mostly because Eli was awkward and didn't know what normal people talked about.

"Where are you living at now?"

Eli nearly groaned in his relief. It seemed Jimmy knew how to make small talk. "I'm renting a room above The Donut Shoppe down the road. It's within walking distance, so it works." Eli finished his sandwich without looking at Jimmy. He hated talking about himself. Anything was better than silence at the moment.

"Are you sick of the smell of pastries?" The heavy laughter in Jimmy's voice had Eli glancing over. He wanted to see the man smiling again. Eli wasn't disappointed.

Biting back an inner happy sigh, Eli shrugged. "It's not that bad. The old lady who runs the place gives me free donuts all the time, so at least I don't starve." Eli looked away again before the final word left his lips. He didn't want to see any pity on Jimmy's face.

"Do you have a phone?"

Eli wadded up his trash and looked for a place to stash it. Jimmy took it from his hand and tossed it in the cooler. Still, Eli couldn't find the courage to look at Jimmy again. "I try to keep up payments on my pre-paid, but sometimes my minutes expire before I can buy more." He fucking hated this. It was as if Jimmy dug for Eli's every secret shame. A card appeared underneath his nose. The logo for Jimmy's bar stared up him.

"The numbers to the bar here in town, the one I own in Nashville, and my cell are all on there."

He owned two bars. Perfect. Could the man get any farther out of Eli's reach? "I'm not a charity case," Eli argued even as he accepted the card.

"That's a first."

Eli's gaze shot to Jimmy's face at the odd statement. "What's a first?"

Jimmy shook his head and chuckled. "I've never had anyone consider getting my number as an act of charity."

"What is this, then?" Eli asked. He couldn't let this continue a second longer without knowing.

With a sigh, Jimmy glanced at his watch before slipping from the truck. Eli blinked at the spot where the man had been sitting behind the wheel only moments earlier. His door opened. Jimmy stood with his hands shoved in his coat pockets, waiting for Eli to get out. Since it was obvious Jimmy didn't intend to answer his question, Eli slid from the truck.

"Thank you for dinner."

Jimmy still didn't respond. With the door standing wide, he took a step forward, backing Eli against the edge of the seat before he could get away. He'd forgotten how huge Jimmy was until the man hovered over him, forcing Eli to crane his neck to hold his stare. "This coat looks familiar," Jimmy said, eyeing the material and tugging at the lapels of Eli's jacket.

Heat flooded Eli's cheeks. "Um. That's because it's yours."

"Huh," Jimmy grunted, looking unfazed. "I wondered where it had gotten off to. It looks better on you anyhow." Tightening his hold on the lapels, he tugged Eli closer, shrinking the gap between them. Eli's mouth went dry. "It's the green," Jimmy explained. "It makes your eyes stand out." With every word, Jimmy moved closer. Without thought, Eli went up onto his toes as Jimmy dipped his head. As they had the night before, their lips met and Eli's mind deserted him. Jimmy's hair fell forward, caressing Eli's face. The scent of citrus tickled his nose. Nostalgia hit with a vengeance. It smelled the same as the shampoo he'd used in Jimmy's shower, the night the man had taken him in. He'd sworn he'd never forget the smell. The odd heat he'd felt in his gut that night, as Jimmy had torn the tag from his shirt, settled inside Eli once more. Back then, he'd been too scared, tired, and hungry to recognize the sensation. Now, he embraced the desire for more from Jimmy.

The sting of Jimmy's teeth sinking into Eli's bottom lip had Eli gasping from the pain. When his lips parted, Jimmy's tongue slipped inside, stroking his. He didn't know what he was doing. For the past three years, he'd been too poor to take anyone out and, before that, too homeless to be of any interest. It was funny how much life could pass a person by while they were concentrating on trying to survive. Every move Jimmy made, Eli mirrored it, hoping the man wouldn't stop. He could barely breathe past the lust clawing at his insides. His hands lifted on their own accord and dipped inside Jimmy's jacket. Without thought, he found his way underneath Jimmy's shirt, going for bare skin. He needed to know how Jimmy felt beneath his fingertips.

Jimmy groaned against Eli's lips. The sound went straight to Eli's cock. "Fuck. I need to let you get back to work. You can't be late."

Work? Goddamn it. He did have that. Jimmy's lips were so full and soft, Eli couldn't resist; he went for them again, craving more. Jimmy let it happen. Maybe he had no clue what he was doing, but Eli knew the man's bottom lip tasted like heaven and Eli couldn't stop drawing it between his teeth, savoring the flavor.

Jimmy broke away. With his forehead pressed to Eli's, he kept his eyes closed. Eli stared at him, memorizing every line.

"You have my number," Jimmy said, reminding Eli of the card Jimmy had given him. "Use it, okay?"

Eli nodded.

With a dip of his chin, Jimmy captured Eli's mouth once more for another kiss before pulling away. "Get back to work."

Since his voice wouldn't work, Eli nodded again before pulling from Jimmy's hold with every bit of regret he felt in his heart. He kept his head down as he headed back inside. The sensation of Jimmy's eyes upon his back lingered until Eli cleared the door. People milled all around him. Eli didn't see a thing. A smile pulled at the corners of his mouth, making his cheeks ache. Chances were good he'd never see Jimmy again. He hadn't forgotten about Jace. But life gave him so few opportunities for happiness, Eli wasn't above grasping for every moment. Jimmy was out of his league and above his reach. The man had issues and Eli had nothing. Still, he wouldn't have traded the past half hour for anything in the world.

As he passed through the door of Hollow Edge, the weight of the world settled on his shoulders once more. This was his place in life, such as it was. He stuffed his coat under the register, determined to get back to it. A worn-looking envelope slipped from the pocket of the jacket and onto the floor. For a moment, he simply stared at it, incapable of moving. When his brain accepted he wasn't imagining things, he bent and scooped it up.

The envelope was sealed and felt lighter than it had been when Eli delivered it to Jimmy. *Maybe he'd kept part of the money?* Eli had been saving that money for a long time. The envelope had been stuffed with ones, five, tens, and twenties, making it thick as hell and straining against its load. This was nothing in comparison. Eli ripped it open. It was still filled with money, except now there was nothing but hundreds. Way more than ten. There was a note on top. Eli pulled it out.

Every time you try returning this money to me, you'll get it back times three. Unless it's your intention to bankrupt me, stop trying to repay me. This is a gift. Not a loan. I need to know you're not struggling. – Jimmy

Eli felt sick. He sifted through the contents of the envelope, doing a quick count. Sure enough, there was three thousand inside. His knees weakened. Why had Jimmy done this? He folded up the money and crammed it in the front pocket of his jeans before anyone spotted it. Walking to and from work every day already made him a target. God forbid anyone know he was carrying around three thousand dollars. Another thought hit. Eli's heart skipped a beat. Had Jimmy only kissed him so he could slip the money in his pocket while Eli was distracted?

Alisha appeared over his shoulder. "Are you okay? You look kind of pale."

"I'm not feeling so great," Eli muttered. His brain didn't want to work right.

She glanced around. "We're pretty dead tonight. Maybe you should go home?"

It wasn't as if he couldn't afford it. There was three fucking thousand dollars in his pocket. The ache in his chest increased. Eli could barely breathe. He should've known Jimmy wouldn't claim he regretted kissing him and then kiss him a second time. Even though things happened fast the night before, that hadn't stopped Eli from getting a good look at Jace. That man was everything Eli wasn't—built, handsome, and closer to Jimmy in age.

"Yeah," Eli said, grabbing his coat and letting Alisha know he hadn't forgotten her. "I think I'll go home. If I'm coming down with something, I don't want everyone catching it." He didn't think stupidity was contagious, but one could never be too careful.

Chapter 3

"I made a cake for you," Annabelle said, sounding chipper.

"But you don't get a slice until you apologize," Karl said, cutting in.

Sam's gaze moved between the two. He looked wary. Jimmy gave himself a quick pat on the back for choosing to hang in the kitchen and avoid the crowd of Sam and Holden's engagement party. Of course, really, this put him closer to the liquor, but he also had good floor seats to the shit show. He covered his mouth, hiding his smile over the worried glint in Sam's eyes. Not that anyone paid Jimmy any attention. People rarely noticed Jimmy unless he announced his presence. It had always been that way. He bled into the background.

Sam cleared his throat. "Did I miss something?"

"Apparently, you missed a few lessons on how to mind your business," Karl said, doing an admirable job of making a man who stood a foot taller than him shuffle his feet like a boy who'd been called to the carpet. "I recently heard a tale about you trying to stick your nose in my son's marriage."

Jimmy settled deeper into his seat. This was one show he didn't want to miss. Everyone knew about Logan's relationship with two men—his husband and their partner. Jimmy thought they were adorable. No one cared what the three men did behind closed doors—except Sam. When Sam had learned of Logan and Malik inviting Ryan to permanently share their bed, he'd lost his shit, showing a puritan side Jimmy never expected. It seemed Logan's parents didn't share Sam's opinion.

"I've let that go," Sam said, trying to explain. "But I spoke up in the first place, because I don't want to see anyone get hurt."

Karl's voice dropped to a deadly level. "My son wouldn't hurt a fly."

Annabelle nodded along. "We raised him better than that."

"Abort," Jimmy mouthed behind Karl, making slashing motions across this throat, but Sam ignored him.

"I didn't want to see him get hurt either," Sam said, keeping up the argument.

Jimmy stood, hoping to make it to cover before the fireworks flew.

A low growl sounded from Karl. "A fly

wouldn't hurt my son if it knew what was good for it."

Annabelle continued to nod, having her husband's back. Malik cleared the kitchen door, bringing all eyes his way. Jimmy sat back down. Sam did what any smart man would do—he threw Malik under the bus.

"Malik and Logan separated for a while last year and didn't tell you," Sam said before running for his life. Malik froze, looking like a deer caught in the headlights.

"I..."

It couldn't have been more obvious Malik didn't know what to say.

Annabelle waved a dismissive hand at him. "Don't worry over it, Malik. We already knew all about it."

Malik's face screwed up in confusion. "You did?"

She nodded, looking confident. "A mother knows these things, and I'm not above snooping. It was obvious Logan was upset all the time. So I called and talked to that pretty blonde girl, Julie, who worked as his assistant at River Night Brewery. She told me everything."

"Oh."

Annabelle snorted at Malik's shocked expression. "Don't look so surprised, babe. I knew you'd work things out. It's like I said—a mother knows." She glanced Jimmy's way, making him realize she hadn't been oblivious to his presence. "Jimmy, are you seeing anyone?"

Eli flashed to mind. "Yes, ma'am," he said even as he wondered why. He wasn't seeing anyone. Jace had dumped him after a short two months together, three weeks ago—thank God—and Eli was... Well, he didn't know yet. Since he hadn't called, Jimmy assumed they were nothing at all—but that kiss. Wow. He couldn't stop thinking about it.

"I bet your mother knows all about him, doesn't she?" she asked, looking confident. Jimmy almost hated to burst her bubble.

"Darling, my momma forgot where she put me when I was eight. FYI, it was where she'd bought her last crack rock, which was a horrible place for a child, in case you were wondering. That's the last I heard of her."

Everyone in the kitchen froze. All eyes turned his way. Since he'd passed three sheets to the wind hours ago, he honestly didn't care.

Annabelle, proving to be the trooper, didn't back down. "So that's a no?"

Jimmy snorted. "Yes, ma'am. That's a no."

Her hands lifted before falling back to her sides. She cast a desperate look around the kitchen. He felt bad for bringing it up. "Why isn't your man here with you or did I miss my introduction?"

Since he'd already ruined one of her points for the day, he smiled and played along. "My invitation didn't say anything about bringing a guest. I didn't want to assume."

Annabelle huffed. "That's bull and you know it. Go get him and get back here before presents at eight."

"Yes, ma'am," Jimmy said, coming to his feet. Before he could get away, she pulled him in for a hug.

She dropped her voice where no one else could hear. "You should've told me about your mom. Not that I should have to tell you this, but you know you have a family right here."

His arms tightened around her. "Yes, ma'am. I know."

She patted his ass. "Go get..."

"Eli," Jimmy supplied.

"Yes, him," Annabelle said. "Get Eli and hurry back, so I can suss him out."

Jimmy pulled away and caught her gaze. "He's shy," Jimmy warned. "Most likely, he'll be too uncomfortable to warm up to anyone right away."

Annabelle scoffed and shooed him away. "Just go get the boy. I won't bite."

With a wink, Jimmy headed out to do as told.

*

Eli stared at his door, wondering what the hell was happening to it. It sounded as if someone was knocking, but he'd never had a visitor before. There wasn't a peephole or window. He had to answer and hope for the best. Sexiness stood on the other side. The impact of Jimmy on Eli's senses never lessened. His blue eyes were a tad bloodshot but were still amazing. The flannel shirt he wore strained against his muscles. Eli had never wanted anyone as badly.

"Hi." Yeah, he knew he sounded like a total dumbass, but it was all Eli had.

"Hi," Jimmy said, sounding every bit as pathetic and easing Eli's mind. "You never called."

Eli held up the science fiction novel he was reading. "Been busy."

Jimmy eyed the worn library book. "I see that. Are you too busy for me?"

At the question, Eli realized he'd made the man stand in the doorway as if he wasn't welcome. Blood rushed to his cheeks as he took a step back. "Sorry about that. I'm not used to having visitors."

Instead of stepping inside at Eli's silent offer, Jimmy snagged the front of Eli's shirt, stopping him from getting away. With the slightest tug, he hauled Eli closer. It was ridiculous how easily Jimmy lured him in. He stood still as Jimmy lowered his head and touched his lips to Eli's. Every time, it got better. There wasn't a need for Jimmy to trick him into opening for him this time. Instead, Eli was the one who deepened their kiss. The taste of wintergreen gum and a hint of whiskey coated his taste buds. Eli's fingers found

Jimmy's hair. The soft locks slid across his palm before Eli tightened his grip and pulled the man closer.

The book fell from his numb fingers before his other hand joined the first. He couldn't get close enough to Jimmy. Jimmy's arms tightened around him. Their bodies collided. Eli moaned. He was turned on to the point of painful.

"This isn't why I came here," Jimmy said as he changed directions and reclaimed Eli's mouth. Eli didn't know why the man had shown up, but he had plenty of reasons for him to stay. "Oh, God. Seriously," Jimmy said, pulling away again, as if it pained him to do so. He looked at Eli like a man on the verge of tears. "Damn. I gave my word I'd be back by eight. Otherwise..." His gaze trailed down Eli's body. He whimpered. Eli didn't have a clue what Jimmy was talking about, but his body didn't care.

"Be back where?" his mouth asked as his body screamed he was a dumbass.

"The party. We're going to a party. An engagement party, to be more specific."

"A party," Eli repeated. "I don't want to go to a party." Did he? Fuck. He didn't know. All Eli knew was Jimmy was there and he was there. They were feet away from his bed, and the man looked at him as if he'd been starving for years. Eli ached for everything Jimmy's stare promised.

"I have to go. It's for some of my closest friends. Well, maybe not my closest. I don't know that I have close friends, but I like the people there. Fuck it. If I have to go, then you have to go."

"Why?" Eli could hear the confusion in his voice, but fuck it. He never had any clue what was going on when Jimmy was involved.

"Because," Jimmy said with a shrug, "I think there's something between us. Annabelle—you'll get to meet her later—asked if I was seeing anyone, and I told her I was dating you. So, you see, in my head, you're already mine."

Eli blinked as his mind went blank. "I'll get my shoes." He turned, ready to do just that when Eli's head cleared enough for other things to slip in. "Hold up." He faced Jimmy once again. "You're dating Jace."

Jimmy's face screwed up in confusion. "No. I told you he dumped me."

Eli searched his mind, coming up blank. "I'm pretty sure you didn't."

As Eli looked on, Jimmy's gaze turned inward, as if running through their conversations in his head. "Huh." Jimmy shrugged. "I honestly don't remember, but yeah, he dumped me a while back. People do that. I'm not long-term material."

"Why?" Eli asked as he stamped into his shoes.

Jimmy shrugged again. "Logan says it's because I'm a drunkard."

"And Logan is..."

"Definitely a close friend," Jimmy answered without missing a beat. "He also manages the bar here in town for me. You'll meet him tonight too."

"So you do have close friends after all?"

Jimmy seemed to think that one over before answering. "At least one."

Eli shoved his arms into his jacket. "You'll regret taking me to this. I'm not good with people."

"I don't want you to be good. Where's

the fun in that?"

Blood rushed to Eli's face. He ducked his head and focused on his shoes, trying to hide his blush. Jimmy's low and sexy-sounding chuckle let Eli know he hadn't missed it. Instead of dwelling on his embarrassment, Eli headed for the door. Jimmy blocked his path, forcing Eli's gaze his way. The man's blue eyes always stole Eli's breath. He couldn't look away.

"I don't think you mentioned your apartment is a studio."

Eli had to swallow past his rapidly drying throat to respond. "I can't imagine why it would've come up."

Jimmy's mouth lifted in one corner. Damn. The man's smirk was so fucking sexy. It almost physically hurt Eli to look at him. "There's a bed right there," Jimmy said, nodding toward it, as if Eli didn't know exactly where he slept each night. "We could skip this. Annabelle would forgive me."

"Would she?"

Jimmy shook his head. A sad smile touched his lips. "Probably not."

To busy himself, Eli scooped his book from the floor and tossed it onto the bed before grabbing his keys and heading for the door once more. "Then we'd better go before you talk yourself into being in trouble."

"I guess you're right," Jimmy said, allowing himself to be led outside. After locking up, Eli fell into step next to Jimmy as they descended the stairs on the side of the building. His gaze landed on the truck sitting in the parking lot as his feet hit the pavement. Realization struck.

"Wait. Did you drive here?"

Jimmy blinked at him, as if Eli spoke a foreign language. "Well, I'm here. My truck is here. How do you think I got here?"

"Oh my God. Give me your keys. I'll drive."

Jimmy passed them over. "Can you drive?"

Eli rolled his eyes as he climbed behind the wheel. "Enough to get my license and a hell of a lot better than some drunk guy."

"I'm not just some drunk guy," Jimmy said, sounding petulant and pulling a hurt face as he buckled his seat belt. "I'm your drunk guy."

Eli pretended Jimmy's claim didn't warm his heart as he continued his lecture. "I cannot believe you drove in this state. You might not care if you kill us, but

I'll never forgive you if you die."

"But you'll forgive me if you die?"

Eli ignored him. The more he talked, the hotter his blood boiled. "Goddamn, Jimmy. What if you'd killed someone's child?"

"This side of you is mega hot."

"Damn it, I'm not joking," Eli said, still bitching as he shifted the truck into drive. "Don't drive again after you've been drinking, okay?"

"This is important to you, isn't it?"

An exasperated sigh escaped Eli. "It's important to almost everyone. Actions have consequences."

A long, loud sigh escaped Jimmy. "Would it make you feel better if I swore never to drink and drive again."

"It would," Eli said without hesitating,

even though he knew any such vow would be a lie on Jimmy's part.

"Fine. I, Jimmy Hale, promise to never drink and drive again. Okay?"

In spite of himself, Eli laughed. Jimmy sounded so sincere—like stating a real declaration. He doubted the man would stick to it, but it made Eli happy to think he might. "Okay. Where are we headed? I'm really driving around town like I know where I'm going."

"I'll get you there," Jimmy said. His words had a definite sexual tint to them. Eli found himself hoping, in spite of all the odds against him, that Jimmy would do just that.

Chapter 4

"This is Eli." Even to Jimmy's ears, he sounded proud to have Eli on his arm. Based on the smiles of everyone surrounding them, they heard the pride in his voice as well.

"Hi, Eli," Logan said, speaking up first. "I'm Logan. In case Jimmy hasn't told you, I manage the local Jimmy's location."

Eli quickly shook Logan's hand. "He's mentioned you. It's nice to meet you."

Jimmy appreciated Logan not pointing out that Jimmy had not ever mentioned Eli. Instead, Logan turned to the man standing on his left. "This is my husband, Malik." Eli shifted closer to Jimmy. It was a subtle move, but Jimmy felt it happen.

He pressed his palm to the small of Eli's back, letting Eli know he'd keep him safe. Eli shook hands with Malik before Logan motioned Ryan's way. "This is our partner, Ryan."

In spite of his best efforts, Jimmy couldn't stop himself from watching Eli's reaction to the introduction. If Eli was surprised, he didn't show it. He smiled kindly as he shook everyone's hand without an ounce of judgment marring his features. The pride in Jimmy's chest grew with each passing second.

When Sam stepped forward, Jimmy expected Eli to scoot even closer. As the World's Strongest Man, Sam was huge, to say the least. He hovered over everyone, taking up more than his fair share of space.

Eli surprised Jimmy. His smile brightened. "Congratulations on your engagement. Your fiancé has amazing eyes. You're very lucky."

Sam blushed and beamed beneath Eli's praise. Annabelle tugged on Jimmy's sleeve, pulling him away from the crowd. With one final glance Eli's way, he ensured the man would be fine before allowing her to completely drag him away.

"Oh my gosh, Jimmy," she hissed the moment they were out of earshot. "He's so gorgeous. I want to put him in my pocket." Jimmy wanted Eli in his pocket too, but he didn't think it was for the same reason as Annabelle. "Can we keep him?"

A low chuckle escaped Jimmy. "You know he's a real person, right? You can't just decide to keep him."

Annabelle scoffed. "You know what I mean. Now that we've met this one, you can't find someone new. We want Eli."

Even as Jimmy laughed, a pain sliced through his gut. No one in their right mind stayed with him for long. Eli would get sick of him. Probably sooner rather than later. "I'm doing my best," Jimmy said for lack of anything more. He glanced Eli's way. Everyone except Sam had wandered away. Sam seemed surprisingly animated with Eli hanging on his every word. As if he felt Jimmy's stare, Eli turned his head. Their gazes met. Eli winked.

Annabelle sighed. "I don't even know what it is exactly," she said as if admitting a dirty secret. "It's like he's almost angelic or something."

Jimmy got what she was saying. Eli was pretty and innocence bled from his pores. Three years ago, when he'd pulled Eli from the dumpster, he'd been nothing more than a dirty kid who called on some long forgotten sympathy inside Jimmy.

Three weeks ago, he'd challenged Jimmy and they'd kissed. Something inside Jimmy shifted. Even he wasn't sure what happened. All Jimmy knew was he couldn't let Eli get away without taking a closer look.

An image of that stuffed and worn envelope passed through Jimmy's mind. It couldn't have been more apparent Eli had scraped and saved for years to repay that money. He could've disappeared. Chances were good they never would've crossed paths again. Still, Eli hadn't given up trying to do right by Jimmy.

"He is an angel," Jimmy said without thought. "One I don't deserve."

Annabelle hugged his arm. "Darling, if anyone deserves someone amazing, it's you."

Before he could argue, she stepped

away and called everyone to the table. It seemed it was time for Sam and Holden to open their presents. It was also the perfect time for Jimmy to reclaim Eli. He didn't know why Annabelle thought he deserved anything good at all, but Jimmy planned to earn Eli.

*

Jimmy's friends were nice. Eli was still uncomfortable as fuck, but that was true of everywhere he went. The longer the night went on, the thinner his nerves stretched. Eli found himself focusing on smaller groups to calm himself. There was some cop there. Eli hadn't caught his name. At least, he didn't think he had. Eli searched his mind, coming up empty. The man standing next to him was definitely named Chance. Eli remembered because he'd thought the name odd. Giving up trying to remember, his gaze strayed toward the threesome in the corner. Even if Logan hadn't introduced his men the way he had, they wouldn't have been able to hide their relationship.

Eli couldn't lie and say he hadn't been shocked. He also couldn't say he wasn't intrigued. As someone who loved a good story, he studied their every move. On the surface, it seemed as if Logan was the centerpiece the other men clung to, but Eli saw deeper. All three men loved one another equally. They took turns eyeing one another when the others weren't looking. There was so much hunger and heat in their gazes, Eli could feel it all the way across the room. They were different in a lot of ways. Malik was big and dark while Logan was small and blond. Ryan was the sexy ginger of men's fantasies. Together, they were fucking hot.

They were also hiding in the shadows,

kissing. Eli couldn't look away. He'd never seen a three-way kiss in real life. Everyone else was too far into their cups to notice. Eli needed to drive Jimmy home. That thought led to another. Where would he stay? Jimmy couldn't drive. They were in his truck. Wow. He hadn't thought this through. As Jimmy had pointed out, his apartment was a studio. There was no living room or couch where Jimmy could crash. Damn...

Malik's fingers curled into the back of Ryan's t-shirt, balling the material into his fists. He pulled, squishing Logan between them. Eli couldn't breathe on the man's behalf. Either that, or watching the three of them had Eli half aroused. He'd given up trying to decide.

"You're staring."

"I can't stop," Eli said, going with the truth.

With a low chuckle, Jimmy stepped between Eli and the three men in the corner, saving Eli from himself.

Even though he could no longer see them, Eli's gaze continued to stray in that direction. "They're beautiful."

"They are." Jimmy's agreement stole Eli's focus. As he met Jimmy's gaze, a smile lit Jimmy's face. "They have nothing on you."

Heat filled Eli's cheeks. Jimmy's smile fell. "Come home with me."

Eli didn't hesitate. "Okay."

"I want to get to know you," Jimmy added, causing disappointment to pour through him.

"Okay." Eli had no idea why he couldn't think of anything more intelligent to say.

"Then I want to learn everything there is to know about your body."

Eli's stomach muscles tensed. "We should tell everyone goodnight."

"Do you still have my keys?"

At Eli's nod, Jimmy linked his fingers through Eli's and tugged him toward where Annabelle, Karl, Sam, and Holden sat eating cake. Everyone looked in their direction at their approach. Under normal circumstances, Eli would've hated having so many eyes upon him. At the moment, all he could focus upon was the way Jimmy's palm felt against his.

"Are you leaving us?" Annabelle asked as soon as they were within earshot.

"We are," Jimmy said, sparing Eli from answering. "We appreciate the invite. Everything was amazing. Congrats again, guys," Jimmy said as he switched his attention Sam and Holden's way. "You're perfect for each other."

The men beamed. Eli's pride swelled. As usual, no one paid any attention to him, but Jimmy's thumb brushed back and forth across Eli's in an absent motion. If anyone had ever held Eli's hand, he couldn't remember it. Jimmy's touch was amazing.

Annabelle focused on him. "It was nice meeting you, Eli," Annabelle said, coming to her feet. Before he could guess at her intentions, she hugged him. Eli flinched but forced himself to stay still. Even once it passed, she didn't completely let go. She held his arms as her gaze moved over his face. His skin burned from the contact. "I can't stop looking at your eyes. They're beautiful. Jimmy is incredibly lucky." With a final pat, she dropped her hands. "Now that you know where to find us, don't stay away."

"I won't," Eli said, even though he wasn't sure if it was the truth. After a few uncomfortable goodbyes, they finally climbed inside Jimmy's truck. Eli didn't realize until they were alone how tense his shoulders had been. He drew a deep breath. His muscles relaxed. Jimmy reached across the space between them and massaged Eli's shoulder.

"Hey, are you okay?"

Eli nodded as he pushed the air from his lungs. He started the truck before Jimmy could ask any more questions. "I need directions."

"Don't worry. I'll get you there." Jimmy ran his hand up Eli's thigh as he made the claim. He nodded straight ahead. "Go to the light and turn right." As Eli did as bade, he could feel Jimmy's stare upon him, scorching his skin. "What's your favorite color?"

A chuckle rose in Eli's throat at the unexpected question. "I've never thought about it."

"How could you not think about it?"

Eli shrugged. "What's yours, then?"

"Take a left up here by the gas station and then turn right at the next light," Jimmy said before answering Eli's question. "It's green. Every shade. It's a peaceful color—like your eyes."

That final point reminded Eli of the one time he'd paid attention to any color. "I guess I like blue. The night you pulled me from the dumpster, as soon as you stepped into the light and I caught a glimpse of your eyes, comparisons ran through my head. That's never happened to me before. So, yeah, I like blue."

A low and sexy laugh rumbled through

the truck. "You like my eyes. I love yours. That settles it. We'd make beautiful babies together."

A surprised bark of laughter escaped Eli at the ridiculous comment. "What's your favorite food?" Eli asked without giving Jimmy a chance to supply the next topic.

"That's easy. Steak."

"Anything Mexican," Eli said before Jimmy could ask.

"Turn up here on the left."

Eli did as told.

"It's the first house. Right there," Jimmy said, pointing out a house with light-colored siding and a two-car garage. As Eli pulled into the driveway, Jimmy stretched across the seat and hit a button attached to the sun visor. The first door slid open and Eli pulled inside. Jimmy hit the button again and the door swept closed behind them, shutting them inside.

Eli killed the engine. Neither of them opened their door. Jimmy shifted in his seat until he sat sideways, focusing his attention on Eli.

"I sleep with the lights on. There're no TVs in my house. I don't vote, because I don't care, and even though I'm great with numbers, I didn't finish school. Everything I have, I earned through blood, sweat, and tears. If I lost it tomorrow, I'd probably be too drunk to care." Jimmy didn't slow. Eli hung on every word. "There're very few people I like, and I most likely wouldn't notice if they fell off the planet. I don't believe in God and can't stand most people who do. In fact, the only prayer I've uttered in years was a plea for a zombie apocalypse to wipe out people of religion. Most people think I'm an asshole. I don't care about that either. The only thing I like almost as much as drinking is working out. I also take part in MMA matches under the Smith Brothers company. Since we met, I can't stop thinking about you." Eli's heart turned over in his chest. Jimmy wasn't finished. "Not even alcohol blurs the image of you in my mind. That's never happened to me before. Even though I never would've believed it, I like it and I want to keep seeing you."

"Okay." There it was again. It was like Eli was a computer programmed with limited speech. He winced at his own dumbassary. Jimmy's chuckle made everything better. An unfamiliar ache in Eli's face made him realize he was smiling. "I don't have a list prepared," he told Jimmy, in case the man expected to hear one. "Sleeping with the lights on doesn't bother me. Very few things put me off my sleep. I don't own a TV either. Not out of any hatred for television. It's just always seemed like an unnecessary expense when I can get books from the library for free. I don't vote because I hate politicians. If I need someone to lie to me, I can talk to myself— no need to make a special effort for it." He tried to remember everything Jimmy had said, so he could give the man the same details he'd shared. He had a feeling he was forgetting a few items. "My parents were religious zealots. That's put me off religion of any kind. I do believe in God, though. That belief gives me someone to talk to other than myself. I don't love anything or anyone, especially me."

He held Jimmy's gaze. "I don't know why you can't get me out of your head, but the feeling is mutual. Although I think you meant since the other night, while you've been in mine for the past three years. I just..." Eli shrugged, searching for a way to explain his thoughts before trying again. "I just want to spend time with you. It doesn't matter what we do. I don't even care if you're sober for it."

Jimmy's mouth lifted in one corner. He snorted. "You're totally unique. Everyone I know is set on fixing me."

Eli's hands lifted of their own accord before falling back to his lap. "I can't fix myself much less anyone else. To me, you're not a project. I don't need one of those, but I want whatever this is happening between us."

"Me too," Jimmy said, making the words sound closer to a vow. "Do you want to see inside?"

When Eli nodded, Jimmy got out. Eli followed. Now that they were headed inside, Eli's nerves set in. They'd been alone before. Hell, they'd been alone for the past half hour. Facts didn't matter to the flutter in Eli's stomach. Jimmy was so much more everything than Eli. At the moment, Jimmy wanted to keep seeing him. Eli was scared shitless that if he stayed much longer, Jimmy would realize how lacking Eli really was. All the fear in the world didn't stop Eli from stepping through the door. The scent of apples and cinnamon hit Eli. His stomach cramped with longing. The place smelled like the home he'd always imagined. After turning off the alarm, Jimmy switched on the lights, revealing a polished kitchen. Wood cabinets and granite countertops called for Eli's touch. He wanted to run his fingertips across every surface. The appliances were all black, blending well with the rest of the kitchen. Eli's gaze automatically sought the source of the delicious smell. A round container of colorful oils caught his eye. Eli moved closer. The aroma increased. He had to stop himself from picking it up and bringing it to his nose.

Jimmy headed for the next room. Eli scurried to catch up. Another light flared to life, revealing a large living room. A sectional took up one quarter of the room and a bookshelf lined one wall. Eli headed straight for it. He'd lied when he'd told Jimmy he didn't love anything. Books were an escape from a harsh reality. He couldn't get enough. Even the way they smelled warmed his heart. Spotting an old and worn-looking novel, Eli pulled it from the shelf. He didn't look at the title before bringing the book to his nose and sucking in a deep breath. Old pages had a certain scent— like dreams.

Jimmy's arms encircled Eli's waist. His chest cradled Eli's back. Eli's eyes shot open in horror as he realized what he'd done. "That's my favorite," Jimmy said, setting his chin on Eli's shoulder. "It's about a man who goes insane watching his neighbor through her window every night. You see, their bedroom windows are next to each other," Jimmy said, warming up to the topic. "He spots her hugging her pillow and crying one night. From then on, he can't stop watching her and creating stories about her life."

"I've read it," Eli admitted, almost hating to ruin Jimmy's story. He loved the sound of Jimmy's voice. It was comforting.

"Really?"

Eli nodded and set the book on the shelf. "Yes. I had a book hangover for two weeks after reading it. Usually, I have endings figured out almost immediately. But, when I got to the end, I was shocked. Never saw it coming."

Jimmy nodded. His chin rocked against Eli's shoulder at the motion. "Yeah. I had no idea it was the woman all along, looking into a mirror, but seeing herself with one of her many personalities."

Eli chuckled. "I started it over from the beginning right away, trying to figure out how I missed the clues."

Jimmy's lips brushed Eli's neck. His eyes fell closed at the sensation.

Fingertips brushed Eli's stomach, skin on skin. He went hard. Lust like he'd never experienced before slammed into him. A pant escaped him. He clenched his teeth to keep it from happening again. Jimmy mouth opened over the cords of Eli's neck. A moan followed the pant. Jimmy's fingertips skimmed the waistband of Eli's jeans. Eli's mind zeroed in on that spot, begging the man to go lower. Instead, Jimmy swept Eli's T-shirt higher. Eli automatically shifted, allowing Jimmy to undress him. Cool air brushed his back as Jimmy tossed the shirt aside and his disappeared as well. When their bare skin met as Jimmy encircled Eli in his embrace once more, a shiver of longing ran through Eli.

"Talk to me," Jimmy begged as he

worked the button loose on Eli's jeans.

"What do you want to hear?"

"Anything," Jimmy said as he sank his teeth into Eli's shoulder.

"I'm pretty sure I'll die if you stop touching me," Eli admitted only because it was the only thought in his head.

Jimmy took his hand and tugged. Eli allowed Jimmy to lead him down the hall. They passed a bathroom and a small bedroom before reaching a larger bedroom. A light flared as they walked through the door before going dim, becoming the perfect mood lighting. Eli found himself hoping the lighting was set to how Jimmy slept and not due to the man bringing home anyone willing to be seduced. The worst part was—when Eli searched his heart—he found he didn't care. He'd take this one night of human touch over nothing any day. It didn't matter if he wasn't important to Jimmy.

After leading him to the edge of an oddly bright-colored bed, Jimmy urged Eli to sit. As Eli looked on, Jimmy slid his zipper down and pushed his jeans down his hips. The man was so goddamn beautiful he almost hurt Eli's eyes.

"You're blushing," Jimmy said as he stripped down to nothing.

Eli could feel the heat in his cheeks, but he wasn't letting any amount of embarrassment stop him. He licked his rapidly drying lips. "Probably."

Jimmy moved to stand between Eli's knees. Tilting his chin up, Eli met Jimmy's stare. "I'm looking right at you. You're definitely blushing. Can I ask you something?"

"Anything," Eli said without hesitation.

"Have you been happy the past three

years?"

He hadn't expected that one. "Ask me something else."

"Are you a virgin?"

Eli's blood ran cold even as he trailed his fingertips down the backs of Jimmy's thighs. "Ask me something else."

"That's what I thought. When is your birthday?"

It was hard to concentrate with Jimmy pushing him onto his back and exploring Eli's body with his mouth. Eli's back arched as Jimmy's lips closed around his nipple. "Damn. Um. It was the day before yesterday."

Jimmy ran his tongue down Eli's ribs. "So you're officially twenty-one. How did you celebrate?"

"When is your birthday?" Eli asked,

dodging.

"Got it. No celebration. It's October 18th," Jimmy said as he worked on stealing Eli's pants.

Eli lifted his hips when prompted. The instant Eli was completely nude, Jimmy backed away, leaving Eli alone on the bed and feeling exposed. His discomfort fled as Jimmy stroked his erection, as if he couldn't resist touching himself while staring at Eli. He moved to the bedside table and grabbed a condom and some lube. Eli watched as he suited up and oiled the outside of the condom before tossing the bottle on the bed. Eli couldn't take the silence.

"Tell me something else about yourself?" he begged.

Jimmy set one knee on the mattress. Eli reached for him. In one quick motion,

Jimmy snagged hold of Eli and rolled. On his back, Jimmy left Eli no other choice than to straddle his hips. Eli lost his breath in the exchange. Seeing the expression Jimmy wore made it hard for him to make his lungs work properly. He looked intense. Almost frightening.

"I don't bottom. Not ever. But don't worry, you're in control here. I won't hurt you."

Eli swallowed. There was something dark behind that confession. Eli owed Jimmy the same. "I don't suck dick. Not ever."

"That's cool," Jimmy said, tugging Eli closer. "I don't need that in my life," Jimmy said before claiming Eli's mouth in a scorching kiss.

I don't need that in my life. Those words. There was so much behind them.

That was something someone said when they saw a future together. All of Jimmy's questions kept running through Eli's mind. Jimmy was getting to know him, just as he'd said, as if Eli mattered. He didn't want to hope. If tomorrow came and Jimmy didn't ever talk to him again, Eli didn't want to regret this. As their tongues clashed, Eli forgot to care about anything at all.

Jimmy's fingertips skimmed Eli's crack. The man's erection probed at his ass. He didn't try forcing his way inside. It was a move Eli appreciated and loathed all in the same breath. His insides quivered in his nervousness. Eli's hands shook from the want. His hips moved of their own accord, letting Jimmy's cock slide between his ass cheeks while they kissed. Their tongues gently touched. Everything about the encounter was sweet rather than torrid. Eli didn't know what he'd been expecting. This wasn't it. He wasn't disappointed. Jimmy made him feel like he genuinely cared. That was more than Eli hoped for. Still, he craved more.

Eli pulled away and set his forehead against Jimmy's. He tried catching his breath. The sensation of Jimmy's erection gently kissing his asshole was making oxygen damn hard to come by.

"Jimmy," Eli breathed, unsure of what he was begging for. At his plea, the blunt head of Jimmy's cock pressed harder against the ring of tight muscles surrounding Eli's asshole. They gave way. It hurt more than Eli expected. A gasp tore from his throat. His muscles tensed.

"Play with yourself, baby," Jimmy urged.

Blood rushed to Eli's face, but he

reached between them and palmed his dick. As the first wave of pleasure ran through him, his muscles relaxed. Jimmy slid an inch deeper. Sweat broke out on Eli's skin. He could do this. Jimmy held still. Eli stroked his cock. Closing his eyes, he concentrated on the sensation.

"That's it, sexy," Jimmy praised and he slid deeper. This time, he pumped against Eli's ass, hitting something that pulled a moan from Eli's throat. His dick leaked, smearing pre-cum across Jimmy's abs. He couldn't pretend he hadn't experimented over the years. There'd been toys in his ass before. Nothing could have prepared him for the real thing. The craving for more was soul deep. Jimmy's expression alone was enough to addict Eli for life. He looked beyond turned on. Knowing he'd been the one to cause Jimmy to look as he did was empowering.

"You're killing me, Eli." At the desperate plea in Jimmy's voice, Eli pressed lower, taking Jimmy deeper until he'd finally taken all of Jimmy. "Are you okay?"

Eli nodded.

"Good," Jimmy breathed before rolling and tucking Eli underneath him in one quick motion. On his knees, Jimmy worked Eli higher before bending at the waist and sucking Eli's crown between his lips. He'd never seen anyone that flexible. In fact, Eli had no idea that could be done. His surprise disappeared in a wave of ecstasy. He forgot to be impressed, as Jimmy pumped against him while Eli's cock brushed the roof of his mouth. He wanted too many damn things to name. All Eli could do was moan as he held on for the ride.

His fingers dug into the sheets,

scratching for purchase. The nerve endings in his dick danced with joy. His skin burned for more. Every muscle in Eli's body tensed. His teeth clenched as he reached for the orgasm looming on the horizon. Jimmy surged forward and captured Eli's mouth. He fisted Eli's cock, pumping to match the rhythm of his dick sawing in and out of Eli's ass. Pressure climbed his shaft, curling his toes. Semen shot from the tip of his cock, coating his skin. Jimmy cried out against Eli's mouth. In that moment, Eli was the most powerful man on earth.

Chapter 5

The best part of the night was the way Jimmy held him. Possibly, cuddling was something people took for granted. Eli hoped he never did. He assumed someone had held him at some point in his life, but Eli didn't remember it. Not that it mattered, since those times wouldn't have been the same as Jimmy holding him. Jimmy's hair clung to Eli's sweat soaked skin. His fingertips skimmed Eli's body. Whispered words of praise brushed Eli's ears. Being with Jimmy, resting in the man's arms; it was the most amazing thing to ever happen to Eli.

Even after Jimmy dozed off, Eli couldn't sleep, absorbing every sensation. He was too pumped to settle down. He felt bad for staring at Jimmy while he slept.

The thought of getting up and doing anything inside someone else's house made him feel worse. Jimmy tried rolling over in his sleep. Eli lifted, freeing him. As much as he hated giving up Jimmy's chest as his pillow, he knew the man's arm had to be numb by now. He'd been holding Eli for hours. Eli rolled too, following him. He wasn't ready to give up Jimmy's body heat. The man was like a furnace. Jimmy's hair had tangled into a mess. It took every ounce of Eli's willpower not run his fingers through it, working out the knots. He loved Jimmy's hair.

Eli chewed his bottom lip, fighting back temptation. His gaze slid down Jimmy's back. The hint of a dark tattoo peeked over the sheet. He'd noticed it earlier when they'd been walking down the hall, but Eli had been too distracted by his lust to take the ink in. Incapable of standing another second, Eli curled his finger around the edge of the sheet, and dragged it down to get a better look. It was a reaper. The tattoo was somewhat disturbing. Eli couldn't pinpoint why it bothered him. He moved the sheet even lower, hoping a closer inspection would wipe away the sick sensation growing in his gut. The reaper covered Jimmy's right side. Its robes flowed around Jimmy's hip.

Tilting his head, Eli tried looking at it from a different angle. The light hit the piece just the right way, revealing a brand underneath the tattoo and above Jimmy's hip. A cold sweat broke out across Eli's skin. A branding would hurt, but right there, it would be excruciating. Yet, Jimmy had the brand covered in ink, as if trying to hide it. They would've had to gone deep with the ink to get his scarred skin to tattoo. It looked as if the brand was initials. Without thought, Eli's fingers brushed the letters, attempting to make them out. He thought they were MS, but he couldn't be sure. Eli's mind raced. Who was MS?

*

A light brush of skin on skin skimmed Jimmy's back. His mind shifted into panic mode. In his half-awake state, everything turned black. The years slipped away until he was in that terrible place. The place he never spoke of. Jimmy sprang into action. In one smooth motion, he flipped, pinning his attacker to the bed. His fingers encircled the man's throat.

Eli stared up him. There was no panic in his eyes. He looked accepting—prepared to die. Reality crept back to him. His finger relaxed. The adrenaline pumping through his veins made Jimmy's insides shake. Instead of trying to explain, he dipped his head and opened his mouth over the slowly fading fingerprints on Eli's throat. His heart raced and blood pounded in his ears. He'd almost hurt Eli. Jesus. He needed a drink. Eli would never forgive him, nor should he.

That thought barely passed through Jimmy's mind before Eli buried his fingers in Jimmy's hair and held him in place. Eli writhed beneath him. Jimmy had to know. His hand slid lower. Eli was hard and ready for him. Jimmy's mood transformed from sheer terror and fury to turned on in an instant. He realized he was probably leaving a hickey on Eli's neck. That couldn't be good for the man's job. Jimmy moved lower, going for his collarbone instead. Eli's inner thighs brushed Jimmy's bare hips as he cradled Jimmy against his body. Their erections bumped. A groan tore from Jimmy's throat.

"Damn, Eli. Run away with me. I'll keep you all to myself on a secluded island."

Eli's grip tightened on Jimmy's hair. "Don't tease me with things I can't have." Jimmy froze. His chin lifted. There was a flush riding high on Eli's cheeks. The man's eyes flashed with heat.

"I'm no tease," Jimmy said, holding Eli's stare. "If ever I make you an offer you're willing to accept, speak up, because I mean everything I say to you."

"Is there an offer open for you to kiss me?"

Jimmy didn't hesitate shooting forward and covering Eli's mouth with his. This man was too fucking amazing for Jimmy. Only moments earlier, Jimmy had been on the verge of snapping Eli's neck, and still, Eli begged for a kiss. Being with

Eli was humbling. They were the relationship he didn't deserve.

"I'm so sorry," Jimmy said between kisses. "Swear I would never hurt you. Swear it," Jimmy repeated, needing Eli to understand he'd never forgive himself for marring this man's skin.

"I'm not afraid."

Eli's claim did nothing to ease Jimmy's guilt. It only took the briefest glance in Eli's eyes to understand the man didn't care if he lived another day. He didn't fear Jimmy, but not for any sane reason. Pulling away, Jimmy held Eli's gaze as he reached between them, palming their cocks. Eli's lips parted on a gasp.

"Ask me for anything. I'd give you the world." It was the least Jimmy could do after almost killing the man. At least, that was what Jimmy told himself. It couldn't be Eli's beautiful eyes and gorgeous soul pulling him in, making him want things he'd never craved before.

"Jimmy," Eli said on a breath.

Jimmy released his dick and concentrated on Eli's. His pleasure didn't matter any longer. This wasn't about sex. It was about survival. Jimmy kneaded Eli's cock as he slipped lower. In his life, he'd been taught a trick or two. He'd learned the only way he could live with the nightmares was to turn them into something good; barring that, he'd drown it in liquor. Today, he had an opportunity to use those skills to tie Eli into knots— addict him to Jimmy's touch.

Before Eli, Jimmy had never touched an innocent. He feared if he did, he'd lose his shit, but it hadn't happened. Instead, hope filled him. Eli felt like a second chance. As Jimmy settled between Eli's thighs, with the man's legs thrown over his shoulders, Jimmy knew just where to start.

Eli's hips left the bed, seeking more, and letting Jimmy know exactly how turned on he was. That was good. He knew Eli would be too sore for sex, but not this. Grabbing the man's ass cheeks, Jimmy spread them wide and dove in. He tongued the asshole that had nearly crippled him hours earlier. A strangled sound came from Eli's throat. Jimmy bit back a smile. He could still remember the first time anyone had tongued his ass. Squeezing his eyes closed, Jimmy pushed the darkness from his mind and focused on the present.

With Eli's ass soaked with spit, Jimmy pushed one finger past the tight ring of muscles surrounding Eli's asshole. He wouldn't try for more. This was about pleasure. It was about addiction. Curling his finger, he found the soft mound inside Eli that would drive him nuts and pressed. Eli scratched at his shoulders. Jimmy smiled as he kept up the torture. He sucked the man's balls between his lips and added to the pleasure. Jimmy intentionally ignored Eli's erection, driving his need higher. By the time Jimmy pressed a light kiss to Eli's cock, Eli cries sounded closer to pain than pleasure. He circled the man's crown with his tongue, swiping away the salty pre-cum. A hum rose in Jimmy's throat as the flavor coated his tongue. Turned-on male was his favorite meal.

Moving slowly, Jimmy allowed Eli's dick to slide across his tongue until it hit the back of his throat. He swallowed him down. His scalp burned as Eli gripped his hair, attempting to hold him in place. Jimmy's cock leaked on the bed. He fucking loved having his hair pulled. That was why he kept it long. For a moment, he forgot his plan to torture Eli. His motions became frenzied. He sucked with no skill. Cheeks hollowed and moans of pleasure surrounding Eli's dick was all he was about. A loud hitched breath bounced off the walls of his bedroom, bringing Jimmy back to reality. Eli's muscles stiffened beneath him as he braced himself for explosion. Jimmy pulled away and tightened his fist on Eli's cock, cutting off the orgasm.

A cry of denial escaped the man beneath him. Jimmy made shushing noises against his stomach, doing his best to soothe him.

"Trust me," Jimmy whispered against Eli's skin. He didn't know if Eli heard. His focus was locked on reading the man's body. Giving a man multiple orgasms was an art. It took perfect timing. The instant Eli's breathing slowed, Jimmy released his hold and swallowed Eli's erection. His throat burned from the abuse. Jimmy ignored it as he allowed the man's cock to saw in and out of his mouth. He kept his cheeks hollowed, intent on one goal—Eli's orgasm. When it hit, semen exploded into Jimmy's mouth, overwhelming him. He lost some hair and skin in Eli's attempt to hang on. The man's orgasm went on and on with Jimmy doing his best to swallow the salty juices filling his mouth. It ran down his chin and onto Eli's stomach.

Jimmy swiped his face on Eli's skin, wiping away the moisture as he climbed the man's body. Eli was limp and gasping for air. Without a qualm, he covered the man's mouth with his, making Eli search harder for oxygen. Their kiss was sweet to the point it made Jimmy's eyes burn. He'd been here before—with a spent man beneath him. An exhausted kiss that held promise of reward. The last time, the only time other than Eli, he'd finished their kiss by slitting the man's throat and walking away.

*

Jimmy sprang from the bed. In his shock, Eli watched the gorgeous male eat up the floor with his stride as he left Eli alone. Jimmy had been hard all over and looked more deadly than Eli had ever seen. His body felt like it was made of gelatin. Eli's brain screamed for him to rush after Jimmy, but his legs wouldn't cooperate. His progress was slow, but Eli made up time by not bothering with clothes. He found Jimmy standing in the kitchen, staring into space. The man's nude body was beautiful. His hard cock stood proud, even if Jimmy's mind was no longer there.

As if snapping back to life, Jimmy threw open the freezer door and pulled out a bottle of Jack. He stared at it. After a moment of studying the bottle, as if it was foreign to him, Jimmy tossed it back inside.

"I have to take you to work, and I swore I wouldn't drink and drive anymore."

Jimmy closed the door and set his forehead upon it. Eli looked on, unsure of what to do or what happened. He startled as Jimmy slammed his head against it, as if trying to beat the monsters into submission. Eli's heart stopped before racing to life again.

He recognized Jimmy's futile act for what it was. So many times in the past, he'd been there. No one could help.

Eli cleared his throat. "My dad used to call me unstable. He said I wasn't right in the head, and that's why he needed to beat the crazy out of me." With his forehead still pressed against the freezer, Jimmy tilted his chin, meeting Eli's gaze, letting Eli know he had the man's attention. "He was right," Eli said, pushing the words past his lips before he choked on them. "You don't know me, Jimmy. Not really. I'm not..." Eli swallowed and tried again. "You're wasting your time with me. If this rage is somehow due to me, you can stop. I'm not worth it." He turned away, determined to find his clothes and a way home. In spite of his addictions, Jimmy was good. Eli had meant every word. He wasn't worth this.

Before he made it three steps, Jimmy overcame him. His arms encircled Eli before hauling him back against his solid chest. He held Eli in place. "This isn't about you," Jimmy said against the shell of Eli's ear. The breath caressing Eli's ear had chill bumps breaking out across his skin. "People say life makes or breaks you," Jimmy continued. "I get up every day and get on with it, but I'm broken. I shattered a long time ago. When people say that, they don't tell you that even demolished, you'll keep living. Beyond all scientific explanation, you keep breathing with lungs that no longer work." Tears pressed at the backs of Eli's eyes. He knew. Jimmy didn't have to say a word. He got it. "Your legs move as they should, even after your knees are taken out from beneath you. Beyond all logic, blood flows through your veins even though your heart is gone. That's what you'll sign on for with me—nothing."

Eli swallowed hard, trying to speak past the huge weight crushing his windpipe. "I've had less than nothing for years. As I said earlier, I'm not afraid."

"So be it," Jimmy said, sweeping Eli's feet from the floor and heading for the bedroom.

Chapter 6

Where the corner met the ceiling in his office held Jimmy fascinated. In truth, he didn't see anything other than an image of Eli in his mind. He recognized he was slowly becoming obsessed. It was out of his control. The poor guy had been so damn tired when Jimmy took him home to change before taking him to work. Jimmy had almost felt bad for keeping the man up all night... almost.

The strong scent of liquor tainted the air, wafting from the bar into his office. Jimmy's muscles clenched. His brain itched and he considered chewing on the edge of his desk like a beaver to give his mouth something to do. He'd had a beer right after dropping Eli off at work. Now, he had less than two hours left before he needed to pick the man up. He couldn't drink.

Logan appeared in the doorway, saving Jimmy from gnawing any furniture in two. As usual, the blond was smiling. He was the happiest person Jimmy had ever met, but seriously, he should be. Jimmy had a bad feeling this shit-eating grin had to do with him rather than Logan's overabundance of blessings.

"So... Eli?"

Yep. He'd called it. Jimmy didn't take the bait. Instead, he waited for Logan to get to the point. Leaning back in his chair, Jimmy crossed his arms over his chest and focused on Logan.

Undeterred, Logan hovered over Jimmy's desk. "Where's he at today?"

"Work," Jimmy said, keeping his voice bland and hoping his joy of talking about all things Eli didn't bleed through.

"Where is work?"

"Hollow Edge."

A line appeared between Logan's brows. "Never heard of it."

"It's a clothing store," Jimmy said, still trying not to smile.

"So..." Logan said again. This time, he trailed his fingers across the top of Jimmy's desk, as if he was trying to appear like he wasn't prying. "How long have you been seeing this guy? I don't think I've ever seen you with anyone. Even when Malik said you were dating some guy from the gym, I never saw a trace of him, but now you're with Eli. I'm not being nosey," Logan said the words fast as if that made them true.

He tried not to laugh. Even though Jimmy was Logan's boss, he considered the man a friend. It would've been odd if he hadn't asked questions. "We've been seeing each other on and off for three years now." Jimmy swallowed down a chuckle as the words left his lips.

Technically, it wasn't a lie. He'd met Eli three years ago, seen him for less than an hour, and then again three weeks ago. The problem was—Jimmy hated when people got in his business. No matter how much he liked them. "Anyhow," Jimmy said, changing the subject as he saw an answer to something that had been bothering him all day. "I'd like to do something special for him for his birthday. Do you have any suggestions? I'm not good at these things."

Logan smirked. "Is it his eighteenth?" Regret passed over Logan's features. He winced. "Sorry. It's not like me to judge. I'm not sure what happened there." Logan cleared his throat, still looking horrified. It was penance enough. "What sort of things does Eli like?"

"Books," Jimmy answered without hesitation. "He loves to read."

"Well, there you go," Logan said as if the matter was settled. "Book lovers are

137

easy to buy for."

Jimmy shook his head. "It has to be more than books. This is important."

Logan's expression transformed, as if he realized how serious Jimmy was about this. "Whoa. Wait. Are you sober?"

Taking the band from his wrist, Jimmy pulled his hair up into a messy bun to avoid looking at Logan as he answered. "Yeah. I have to pick Eli up from work in a couple of hours."

"Whoa," Logan repeated. He sat. The way Logan stared at him had Jimmy's skin crawling.

"If you're not helping me, then get back to work. I don't need freeloaders."

Logan pulled a face. "Damn. I like drunk Jimmy better."

Jimmy blew out a breath. "Yeah, well, I do too, but I won't risk Eli by drinking and driving."

Logan's mouth fell open. "Holy shit.

Jimmy... you need an awesome gift for this man's birthday."

An exasperated sigh escaped Jimmy. "That's what I've been saying for the past twenty minutes. Way to keep up, Logan. Obviously, I'm not paying you enough."

"No need to get bitchy," Logan muttered under his breath. "Okay, so, he likes books. Let's start there. Who's his favorite author?"

"T.L. Crisp." Even Jimmy blinked at how quickly that piece of knowledge came to the surface.

Logan leaned forward and pulled his cell phone from his back pocket.

"So much for my no cell phone policy," Jimmy bitched with no real heat.

"Hush," Logan said without looking at him, as if he was the boss and not Jimmy. He played with the device in his hand for a minute. A smile exploded across his face. "Here we go. Talk about serendipity.

T.L. Crisp is signing books tomorrow at the Atlanta Fulton Public Library. That's like a three-hour drive from here. You should make a night of it. Drive down tonight. Get a room—preferably a nice one—and go to the signing tomorrow. Make the whole trip all about Eli. Nothing is more precious than time together, showing care for his interests."

Jimmy thought it over. Logan's plan wasn't as grand-scale as he hoped, but he had to admit, it was a sweet one. "I like this." He pushed to his feet before Logan could say anything more. "If I want to pull this off, I have a ton of shit to do before Eli gets off in two hours."

"Go. I've got things covered here."

Jimmy shoved his phone in his back pocket. "I know you do. That's what I pay you to do."

"Damn. I still like drunk Jimmy better."

Since Logan didn't sound upset, Jimmy headed for the door. "I still do too," he muttered under his breath. Before he made it outside, Jimmy turned and focused on Logan. "Don't take it personally. You know I love you."

Logan pushed the chair back on two legs and glanced over his shoulder at Jimmy. "I know. That's why I put up with you."

Jimmy bit back a laugh. "I'll add fifty dollars to your check this week if you don't tell Malik and Ryan I'm sober today."

"That piece of gossip is worth more than fifty."

"Greedy fucker," Jimmy said with no real heat.

"Bitch," Logan tossed back, sounding way too pleased with himself.

It wasn't until Jimmy climbed behind the wheel of his truck that he realized he was smiling. Not only that—Jimmy was genuinely happy for the first time in years.

*

He couldn't stop smiling. All day, Eli had tried wiping the ridiculous grin from his face. It wouldn't go away. For the thousandth time, Eli tried rearranging his features into some semblance of maturity. It didn't work.

"Someone looks happy today."

At the sound of Jimmy's voice, the crazy smile somehow managed to grow even bigger. Hope was a hard thing to beat into submission. In his life, Eli had never possessed so much of that emotion.

"Hey," Eli said, sounding every bit as excited to see Jimmy as he felt.

"Hey yourself." Jimmy set his elbows on the counter and lowered his voice for Eli's ears alone. "I've never been more tempted to kiss someone and get them fired in my life."

The world fell away. "I could clock out five minutes early, then what could they say?"

Jimmy straightened away. "I'll wait."

Eli headed for the back to clock out, biting his lip to hold back his smile. Still his cheeks pulled, battling it out.

Alisha blocked his path to the clock. "I have to know. Is that your boyfriend? I started to ask when he stopped by a few weeks ago but decided to mind my business. Now it's over. I have to know," she repeated.

The laughter escaping Eli had as much to do with his happiness as it did Alisha's question. She'd worked by his side for almost two years. Even though they weren't close, Alisha was the closest thing he had to a friend.

"Yes. That's him."

Her jaw dropped. As she visibly floundered for a response, Eli stared at her dark skin, wishing for the millionth time he had her flawlessness. "Wow, Eli. He's... Holy shit."

Eli wondered if a person could hurt themselves from smiling too hard. "I know."

"Well, damn. Get to clocking out then. You need every minute of that."

"Agreed," Eli said, sounding breathless even to him as he stepped around her and scanned his time card. He moved to rejoin Jimmy. Alisha called out, stopping him.

"One day soon, I expect all the details. You understand?"

Eli dipped his chin, acknowledging her words even as he prayed that day never came. There were some things he never intended to share. How he'd met Jimmy was one.

*

Jimmy was damn near to dancing in place by the time Eli reappeared. His level of happiness had hit ridiculous upon seeing the man again. Eli's maroon-colored sweater and khakis molded to his skin, revealing a package Jimmy wanted to unwrap. The smile he'd been wearing when Jimmy walked into the store had him ready to jump the counter and claim the man's mouth. As he watched Eli crossing the room, Jimmy had to force himself to wait.

When Eli reached his side, Jimmy couldn't contain his excitement a second longer. "I have a surprise for you."

Eli's face screwed up in confusion. The

way his nose curled had Jimmy chewing on the inside of his cheek from the want. "A surprise? For me? What kind of surprise?"

Something evil rose inside Jimmy. As much as he wanted to see Eli's reaction to his birthday present, he also wanted to torment the man a little. "You'll see." He hadn't meant his tone to be quite so cryptic, but there it was.

"That sounds ominous," Eli said as he slipped his arms inside his coat. "Will I like this surprise?"

"I hope so." Worry ate at Jimmy's gut. He wasn't joking. It hadn't occurred to him until now that Eli might not be interested in going out of town with him. Maybe he'd overstepped his bounds? Jimmy shrugged it off. He definitely had overstepped. Fuck it. That was him. He was always to the extreme. Best to find out now if Eli couldn't handle it. Taking Eli's hand, he rushed the man from the store.

"Are we in a hurry?"

"Yep," Jimmy said, heading for the exit. He'd snagged a good parking spot. All he had to do was get Eli there. He needed Eli's kiss like oxygen. "I want you to myself." The moment they reached the truck, Jimmy rushed Eli inside. After climbing behind the wheel, Jimmy threw himself in Eli's direction, absorbing the man's laughter as if it was his life's breath. The sound died on a sigh as their lips met. Eli's fingers immediately found Jimmy's hair. He tugged, making Jimmy's scalp sting. Jimmy craved everything and he wanted it right then. Eli's tongue curling around his wasn't enough. He needed to get closer.

With a groan, Jimmy pulled away and tried getting ahold of himself. They had a long drive ahead of them before he could play. First, he needed Eli to agree... Rather, he needed Eli to accept they were headed out of town. Reaching behind the seats, he grabbed the overnight bag he'd bought at a store in the mall and handed it to Eli.

"Your surprise."

Eli shook the bag. "I'm already loving the gesture. What's inside?"

Exasperation had Jimmy rolling his eyes. "Open the damn thing and find out."

After unzipping the bag, Eli shifted through the contents as if he thought there might be a snake inside. Jimmy had never seen anyone look more nervous while receiving a gift. "You got me two sets of clothes and toiletries. Not that I'm complaining, but that's an odd gift."

"Read the card," Jimmy said, near to

bouncing in his seat.

Eli tore open the envelope like a man scared to rip anything. "It's a birthday card," Eli said, sounding amazed. Jimmy didn't comment. He was too busy holding his breath. Eli flipped it open. His eyes moved from side to side, skimming over the contents. He snagged the folded up papers inside and opened it. "It's a hotel reservation and a flyer for a book signing," he said, pointing out the obvious. His tone gave away nothing.

Jimmy nodded. "T.L. Crisp is in Atlanta, signing copies of his new book tomorrow. I got us a room near the library. If we get up early enough, we could be first in line."

The way Eli stared at him could've meant anything. There wasn't an ounce of emotion on his face. "We're going on a trip?"

149

Jimmy dipped his chin. Wariness set in. "Just an overnight one. Unless you want to stay longer," he added. "But I wasn't sure if you had to work tomorrow or if you were willing to call in." Worry sat heavily on Jimmy's shoulders. He hadn't thought things through. Eli probably couldn't afford to take off work. Jimmy was more than willing to give Eli the money he'd miss by missing a day's pay, but Eli wasn't likely to accept. He chewed on his bottom lip, unsure of what to say.

"I've never been on a trip," Eli whispered before pushing the bag into the floor and launching himself at Jimmy. Eli kissed Jimmy's face, starting at his lips before going for both cheeks and eyes. From there, he pressed his lips to Jimmy's chin before covering his forehead in light kisses. Jimmy's heart swelled. His stomach hurt from laughing. "Thank you,"

Eli said, sounding out of breath.

Jimmy couldn't take anymore. He needed the flavor of Eli's skin coating his tongue. Pushing, he worked Eli back across the truck and into his seat. Working at double task, he licked a path down Eli's neck and until he reached the man's shoulder. As he did so, he pulled the seatbelt loose, strapping Eli into his seat. He had to get this truck moving soon before they went to jail for indecency. Jimmy couldn't move away without copping a feel. He stroked Eli's cock through his pants as he captured the man's lips. As their tongues met, Jimmy made himself a thousand promises. One stood out from the rest—he would let himself be happy. No more self-destruction or thinking he wasn't good enough. This man, he deserved a real shot at life. Eli had missed out on so many things other people took for granted. It was his turn in life. Since there was no way Jimmy could give up Eli, he'd have to get his shit together.

With a final brush of lips on lips, Jimmy pulled away. "I know you're tired, baby," He said, swiping the moisture from Eli's bottom lip before moving away. "It'll take a little more than three hours to get there, so kick back and get some sleep. It might be the last chance you get for the night," Jimmy added as he fired the truck to life.

*

Eli hadn't been lying about nothing putting him off his sleep. When Jimmy had given him permission to kick back, he'd done just that and slept the entire way. Now that they'd made it to their room, Eli was up for anything. Jimmy, not so much. He looked wilted in a way Eli hadn't seen before. He had a bad feeling it had nothing to do with not sleeping.

"We passed a bar downstairs," Eli said as he tossed his bag on the bed. "Do you want to run down and grab a drink?"

The way Jimmy's mouth lifted in one corner made Eli's stomach muscles clench. He was as easy as that when it came to this man. It didn't help that Jimmy was the most amazing person on the planet. He'd already done more for Eli than anyone else ever had, and Jimmy did things as if they meant nothing. No way could he understand how he rocked Eli's world. The least Eli could do was keep him company while he drank.

"Do you drink?" Jimmy asked. "I haven't seen it yet."

Eli shrugged. "Although I can't say I haven't ever, not really, no."

Jimmy leaned his shoulder into the wall next to the bathroom. "Yet you still want to go get a drink?"

Eli considered the humor in Jimmy's voice before answering. He wasn't sure of Jimmy's mood. There was something lying in wait just below the surface. "For you? I'm almost scared of what I'd do," Eli said, deciding to go with honesty.

Jimmy straightened away and took a step in Eli's direction. "Would you let me hold you?"

It was Jimmy's tone—like his question had been more of a threat. All of his senses sharpened. "Anytime you like."

The gap between them became smaller as Jimmy moved even closer. "I think you say things you don't mean. What if I showed up at three in the morning, wanting nothing more than to climb into your bed?"

"You know where I live," Eli said, taking a step back without thought. Jimmy overcame him. The backs of his knees hit the mattress. He sat. Jimmy kept moving forward until he had Eli flat on his back. The man crawled on top of him. Eli stared up at Jimmy—dry mouthed and empty headed. Sometimes Jimmy seemed deadly. Instead of sending Eli running for the hills, he wanted more.

"I want to hold you right now."

"You are," Eli said, pointing out their current state.

Jimmy shook his head. "This isn't me holding you." He shoved Eli's bag to the floor before plopping down full weight onto Eli.

Jesus. The man was heavy. Eli shook with silent laughter. He couldn't draw a breath to make a sound. Jimmy rolled his weight to his hip, giving Eli room to breathe without actually moving away. With his face buried against Eli's throat, Jimmy sang "Happy Birthday" to Eli. Eli blinked, telling himself it wasn't tears pooling in his eyes. Life had been so damn cruel, and then Jimmy had appeared. He wasn't blind. Jimmy was fucked up— probably more than Eli. There was also something equally beautiful about the man holding him. What he'd told Jimmy the night before held true. He wasn't afraid. Jimmy couldn't break his heart. The shattered mess inside his chest had been that way long before Jimmy came along.

"Make a wish."

A snort left Eli without his permission. "Doesn't the making-a-wish part come after blowing out candles, or something like that?"

Jimmy leapt from the bed and crossed the room to where he'd left his overnight bag on the dresser. "Oh, yeah." Eli watched as Jimmy dug around inside. He came out with a plastic grocery bag. Eli tried peeking around his shoulders, but Jimmy kept shifting his stance and blocking his movements from sight. Finally, the man turned. Jimmy held a small cake with a candle that said "twenty-one" stuck in the center. The candle was lit. Its flickering light had nothing on Jimmy's smile. He was proud of himself.

"Now you can make a wish."

Eli scooched to the end of the bed. He held Jimmy's gaze as he leaned forward and blew out the candle. In his life, Eli had made a lot of wishes. Every time the clock struck eleven-eleven or a star fell from the sky, Eli would close his eyes and cast his aspirations to the imaginary beings in control of such things. This was the first time he'd ever believed there was a real shot of his wish coming true. Just being with Jimmy gave Eli hope for the impossible.

Chapter 7

Three months later...

"I have to go to the Nashville location tonight."

"Okay," Eli said, sounding as if he wasn't concerned.

"If I could avoid it, I would. There's no way I'll be back in time to get you from work."

Eli nodded as if it was unimportant, raising Jimmy's hackles a hair more. "That's fine. I can walk home."

Jimmy growled. He didn't mean for it to happen. The sound rose in his throat and escaped past his lips before he could swallow it down. All this goddamn not drinking was murder on his mood. He couldn't stop.

"You could at least act like you care something terrible could happen to you on your way home or that you won't be seeing me after work."

Eli eyed him. His expression gave nothing away. "Tell me what you want me to say, and I'll say it. I don't know what you're after."

Goddamn it. He was after some fucking emotion—some clue he wasn't alone in this inability to be apart. Instead of digging out some bravery and saying that, Jimmy allowed his temper to rise.

"For fuck's sake, Eli. Nobody wants a goddamn puppet. If I wanted my words repeated back to me, I'd buy a motherfucking parrot." His voice rose with every word. Jimmy didn't mean for it to happen. With his hands on the wheel and his gaze fixed upon the road, Jimmy didn't have to look at Eli. That made it easier for him to be a dick. Eli didn't respond. The light turned red and Jimmy glanced his way. The man's hands were curled into fists in his lap. His knuckles were white and his jaw was locked. He stared straight ahead—motionless. Regret slammed into Jimmy, stealing all the air from inside the truck. He'd always known he was the worst sort of bastard bred from the scum of the earth. In all his life, he'd never thought less of himself than he did in that moment. Eli had been trying not to argue. That was his only crime.

"I'm sorry I don't give you what you need," Eli said, sounding hoarse.

Jimmy wondered if he could pull off running himself over with the truck. He dug the heels of his hands into his eye sockets, waiting for the light to turn green.

The hint of irritation, scratching at Jimmy's brain, wanted to point out that was literally the stupidest thing he'd ever heard. Thankfully, Jimmy wasn't a complete idiot. Before Jimmy could think of a reasonable response, Eli broke the silence.

"On the nights I don't get to see you, I sort of putter around listlessly. I no longer know how to function without you. The thing is, I don't want you feeling guilty for having to work, and I damn sure don't want you thinking I'm needy. But yeah, I miss you and I wish you could be with me every night. I'm also not helpless." He met Jimmy's gaze. Fire blazed in his eyes. "And I absolutely know what bad things can happen to people on the streets late at night."

Jimmy realized something important. He should've stepped up his game in regard to their relationship. Jimmy held on to all the words racing through his head. The instant Jimmy put the truck in park at Eli's work, he was across the seat and holding Eli. He felt Eli's muscles relax as he engulfed the man in his arms. Jimmy loved the way he immediately melted.

"Baby, I'm so sorry. Please ignore my bullshit. I don't know why I say shit I don't mean sometimes. Missing you puts me in a shit mood."

Eli's arms tightened around Jimmy. "Why are you missing me? I'm right here."

A chuckle escaped Jimmy. "I can't crawl under your skin, that's why."

"You are under my skin," Eli said against Jimmy's shoulder. "Haven't you been feeling shorter lately? How's your appetite?"

Jimmy's body shook with laughter.

Eli didn't stop. "As a matter of fact, if you're going to be taking care of my skin from now on, we need to have a discussion about lotions. I like cocoa butter, but not the cheap shit that comes out runny. You have to use the thick stuff you can smell a mile away."

"You're ridiculous."

He felt Eli shrug. "You're the one who wanted under my skin, and you're there, Jimmy. I don't want to work or pay bills. Adulting sucks and I feel like I've been doing it for a million years with no relief in sight. You're the only good part of my day. I didn't realize you didn't know that already."

Jimmy was equal parts happy and guilt ridden. If he was the best part of Eli's day, he'd done a great job of ruining it today. "In the future, I'll try harder to ask for what I want. Instead of acting like a dick."

"Sometimes I think we're learning together."

Jimmy pulled away and met Eli's gaze. Wariness rose inside him. "What do you mean?"

Eli shrugged, looking uncomfortable. "No one has ever cared about me, so I don't know how to keep that going." He paused, and Jimmy held his breath. "I get the feeling no one has ever cared about you either, not the way I do."

He'd never wanted to know anything as badly. The temptation to ask Eli how much he cared was eating at Jimmy's insides, but he was scared. If asking meant revealing he'd never been loved by anyone or anything, then he couldn't do it.

Maybe he was weak, but there it was. He knew Eli had gone through some shit in his life, but it was nothing in comparison to his bullshit. Jimmy couldn't set that at Eli's feet. He wouldn't sully Eli with that. Instead, he kissed Eli goodbye while holding tight to the knowledge the man cared about him. It was enough.

*

Jimmy's horrible mood weighed heavy on Eli's mind. Sometimes he wondered if he was enough for Jimmy. Maybe he didn't have what it took to hang on to him. He didn't doubt for a second that Jimmy had lived through something horrible Eli didn't understand, but he also didn't feel secure enough to ask what that something was. It was also possible he was better off not knowing.

Eli's steps slowed as he hit the parking lot, leaving work. Ryan stood, leaning against an Accord and waiting.

"Hey," Ryan said, sounding bright. "Jimmy asked me to give you a ride home."

Eli shuffled his feet. He knew it would be rude to refuse after Ryan had driven there and obviously had been waiting for Eli to get off work, but damn. He could almost see his apartment from where they stood.

"Thank you. I don't live far." Eli put the words out there, in case Ryan had somewhere else he'd rather be.

"I know. Jimmy told me you live above The Donut Shoppe. I love that place. Reckon they're still open?"

The hopeful note in Ryan's voice had Eli accepting the ride. "Yeah. They don't close for another hour. Of course, all the good stuff is probably gone by now."

"It's all good in my book," Ryan said, opening the door for Eli—like a gentleman.

Eli chanced a smile. "I'll grab you something when we get there. The owner, Jasmine, gives me the leftovers almost every night. I don't always eat them. Really, you can only eat so many donuts, but her kindness counts with me."

"Awesome," Ryan said, as he pulled from the parking lot.

Eli couldn't stop staring at the man's profile. He was a friend of Jimmy's. Even though Eli didn't know how long they'd known each other, the man had to know Jimmy well enough for Jimmy to send him to get Eli. There was a certain level of trust in knowing you could count on someone that went into that. That meant, surely, he knew a few things about Jimmy that Eli didn't.

"Is it okay if I ask you something?"

Ryan sighed at the question. "Yes. I am completely happy being the unmarried one in a three-person relationship."

Eli's mind went blank. "Um, okay. I'd actually planned to ask you how long you've known Jimmy, but all right."

"Wow," Ryan breathed, sounding embarrassed. "I'm so sorry. Ever since Sam made it clear he doesn't approve of me being with Malik and Logan, I'm overly sensitive about the matter. I feel like a total dumbass now."

"Don't," Eli said, shaking his head. "Even though I don't know what it's like to have friends, I—"

"Wait," Ryan said, holding up a hand and interrupting Eli. "How do you not know what it's like to have friends?"

169

Eli shrugged. "I didn't grow up in the kind of home where you invited people over. By fifteen, I was living in the streets, and..." Eli shrugged again. "I don't know. My life hasn't been conducive to building relationships." Eli waved off the topic. "Anyhow, I can imagine having someone close to you reject your relationship would make you less likely to invite others in, but you should know, Sam's reaction had nothing to do with you. After his niece died, his brother spent all his time drinking and cheating on his wife. Sam saw what it did to her, having her husband inviting strangers into their marriage, stealing their shared grief. Sam feels that if he'd never started down that path, he'd still be alive. It's given him a jaded outlook on relationships that challenges his beliefs."

Since Eli only lived a few minutes from

work, Ryan had pulled into the parking lot of The Donut Shoppe while Eli had been giving his speech. Now Ryan sat staring at Eli as if he'd sprouted wings.

"How could you possibly know all that?"

Eli twisted his fingers in his lap. He hated when people looked at him like he was a freak. "I stood still at the engagement party, and he told me. You should talk to him too. Let him know his support is important to you, and he let you down."

"I didn't say that."

"You didn't have to," Eli shot back. He grabbed the door handle, prepared to sprint. "Even though I didn't need it, thank you for the ride." Before Eli could get out, Ryan set his hand on Eli's forearm, stopping him. Eli jumped as if he'd been burned. Ryan dropped his hand. His horrified expression made Eli wish for death.

Ryan kept his hand extended as if attempting to mollify Eli after his over-the-top reaction. "Sorry. I just wanted to say— I've known Jimmy for a few years, but I don't know why he is the way he is, if that's what you'd planned on asking earlier. As far as I know, no one knows what drives him."

Eli nodded, still trying to recover from being touched. "Thank you," Eli said. His voice came out unsteady. Without a backward glance, Eli leapt from the car before he gave Ryan more reasons to think he was crazy. He quickly reversed course and opened the door again. "Don't leave yet. I promised you donuts." That was the only reason he'd gone back, Eli swore to himself as he headed for the shop. It was his way of saying thanks for the ride, and then they could pretend as if Ryan hadn't caught a glimpse of his unbalanced side. Hopefully, they'd also never see each other again.

*

Eli's apartment was ridiculously easy to break into. Plus, the man slept like the dead and had no sense of self-preservation. Jimmy hadn't tried to be quiet. Eli hadn't budged. After a quick glance around, he pulled his shirt over his head, shucked his pants, and climbed into bed with Eli.

"You're like a herd of buffalo."

A chuckle escaped Jimmy as he realized Eli had been awake the whole time. "Apparently, you're fine to lie here and get killed by an intruder."

"I knew it was you," Eli said, motioning

toward the window by the bed. "I heard you pull in."

Jimmy curled himself around Eli and held on. "Why didn't you come unlock the door for me?"

Eli huffed. "I expected you to knock. You know, like a normal person? If you notice, I turned the light on for you."

Since Jimmy had no intention of apologizing for being himself, he changed the subject. "There're two coffee cups sitting out."

Eli rolled onto his back, meeting Jimmy's gaze. "You sounded really jealous right then. It was hot."

Jimmy couldn't deny it. Instead, he waited for Eli to explain the cups.

Eli sighed. "Ryan stayed for a while after he brought me home. Thanks for worrying about me getting home, by the way."

"You're mine. It's my job to worry."

The way Eli's mouth turned up in one corner at the claim had Jimmy's mouth going dry. He knew he sounded possessive, but he was. There was no hiding it. "What made Ryan decide to stay? I would've expected him to rush home to his men."

"They're out of town. Malik had a fight tonight in Washington. Ryan has to work tomorrow, so he couldn't go," Eli said, explaining everything. "We were discussing the best way for him to talk things through with Sam."

That made sense. There had been a lot of tension in the air since Sam had shown an unexpected Puritan side. "Did you get anything figured out?"

"I hope so," Eli said, sounding thoughtful. "All of your friends seem nice. It's best if they stick together."

"They're your friends too."

Eli smiled. "That's nice, but we both know that isn't true. If you dump me tomorrow, they'd forget me in less than a week. Plus, I think I freaked Ryan out a little."

Jimmy tried hard to listen. With Eli's body against his and the man's scent tickling his nose, Jimmy's mind kept drifting from the topic. "How did you freak him out?" Jimmy asked as he dipped his head and kissed Eli's neck.

Eli tilted his chin up, giving Jimmy better access to his throat. "He touched me," Eli answered with lust tinging every word.

Jimmy's head shot up. "What the fuck

was he doing touching you?"

There was already a flush on Eli's cheeks from Jimmy's small kiss alone. The sight almost cooled Jimmy's temper— almost.

"My arm," Eli explained. "He touched my arm, trying to get my attention. I didn't like it."

Jimmy settled back down. "That's okay, babe. He didn't understand, and next time, he'll think twice before reaching for you."

Eli chewed on his bottom lip. The move had Jimmy wanting to taste it as well. "I don't understand either," Eli said, sounding lost. "My whole life I've been odd, and..." Eli's expression broke Jimmy's heart. "Why can't I stop being the crazy one?" Eli whispered the question, as if ashamed.

"Baby you're not crazy," Jimmy said, doing his best to soothe him. "If I had to venture a guess—I'd say you're slightly autistic, and your parents didn't know how to handle that."

Eli rolled his eyes. "Did you just pull a medical condition out of your ass and diagnose me with it? You're not a doctor. How could you possibly know that?"

Blackness coated Jimmy's brain, threatening to pull him into a place he didn't want to go. He tried shoving the sensation away for Eli's sake. "It used to be my place to observe kids." He couldn't do this. Jimmy sucked in a deep breath and tried a different tack. "You're right. I'm not a doctor. Just think about it, okay? You hate loud places and shy away from people's touch. Except mine," Jimmy added, sounding cocky even to his ears. "And even though you try to fight off your

OCD ways, I see you struggling not to line your shoes up perfectly every time you take them off. My guess is, you're only borderline, but there's nothing wrong with that or you. So stop saying you're crazy."

Eli bit his bottom lip again, making Jimmy's stomach growl. "You've never seen my temper snap when I can't take anymore."

The struggle not to smile was real. He knew Eli was serious, but Jimmy kind of wanted to see that side of Eli. He'd bet good money it was sexy. "I'm not afraid," Jimmy said, using the same words Eli had the first time he'd seen Jimmy's ugly side. "I'll take you any way I can have you. Even enraged and out for blood, you're a thousand times better than anyone I've ever met."

"Three months isn't a long time. You could change your mind."

179

"Three months is an eternity with me." Shifting positions, Jimmy rolled Eli beneath him before settling down between the man's thighs. "I'm hard to tolerate, Eli. You make it look easy. In fact, I think you should move in with me."

Eli's expression went a step beyond comical. "Shut up," he said, sounding exasperated. "You're a cruel tease."

"I'm being one hundred percent serious, Eli. After I dropped you off at work, I had a small panic attack thinking about you walking home alone, and me not being here for you." Jimmy searched Eli's face before admitting something he hadn't fully accepted for himself. "I don't think I can quit drinking and worry over where you are at night at the same time."

"Nobody asked you to quit drinking."

"I know."

Eli searched his face as if assessing his seriousness on the matter. "Your house is too far away for me to walk to work."

"I'll take care of that," Jimmy said, rushing to reassure him. "I'll take care of everything." He'd make any promise it took to get Eli to agree.

"What if you decide you don't want me anymore? I'll be back in the street."

Jimmy's face hardened. He felt it happen. "I will never let you live in the street again. Ever. Do you understand me?" Jimmy leaned down, going nose to nose with Eli. His hair fell forward, surrounding their faces and creating a small place for them alone, cutting them off from the world. It was only the two of them—no one else. For Jimmy, it seemed symbolic.

"Yes," Eli said, whispering the word as

181

if he felt the same seclusion Jimmy did and didn't want to disrupt it.

His fingers curled around the waistband of Eli's underwear before dragging them down one hip. "Say you'll come home with me to stay."

"Okay," Eli said, bringing a roar of triumph racing through Jimmy's blood.

"I'll take care of you, baby," Jimmy swore as he peeled the clothing from Eli's body. "Nothing bad will ever happen to you again," he promised as he settled his lips upon Eli's stomach. "You'll see," he whispered against Eli's hipbone as he dragged his teeth down Eli's body. Eli's fingers found Jimmy's hair and held on. His ragged breaths filled the room and Jimmy hadn't touched the man's cock yet. "Eli." The name tore from Jimmy's throat but came out hoarse against Eli's skin. "Even when there are a million people around, the only time I'm not alone is when I'm with you. That's when I'm whole." Lust burned though Jimmy's veins, but tears stung the backs of his eyes. For years, he'd been numb. He'd intentionally stayed that way. Eli appeared in his life, bringing with him a sliver of hope. Once Jimmy let that ray in, Eli had burst in, giving Jimmy life for the first time in memory. He'd spent his life searching for someone perfect—someone who would make him clean. It had never crossed his mind he needed something else entirely—someone like him.

Now Eli had agreed to live with him. Jimmy couldn't play at getting his shit together any longer. He had to succeed. His tongue found Eli's erection. A gasp bounced off the walls of the tiny apartment.

"That's it, baby," Jimmy praised before

swallowing the man's cock. Eli might be shy and blush a lot, but he always claimed what he wanted when Jimmy offered. His fingers tightened on Jimmy's hair. He openly fucked Jimmy's mouth.

"Damn, Jimmy."

Jimmy pulled back, intent on torturing him. "Tell me what you want," he demanded while Eli writhed beneath him.

Eli tugged, urging Jimmy higher. "Come here, please."

He couldn't make Eli beg. It hurt his chest when he did. Jimmy didn't stop climbing until their mouths clashed. Eli matched his every stroke as he pushed at Jimmy's underwear.

"Tell me what you want," Jimmy begged.

"Your hot cum coating my skin while

your scream my name."

Jimmy's blood ran cold. He tried wrestling the material away from Eli. "You don't want that, baby. Ask for something else."

As if sensing Jimmy's panic, Eli shushed him. "Shh, it's okay."

Jimmy froze. He held Eli's gaze. The man didn't look upset. He pushed Jimmy's underwear past his hips, setting his erection free. Jimmy let it happen.

"I don't want to get you dirty." Even to his ears, Jimmy sounded desperate.

Eli's expression said he heard what Jimmy meant rather than what he said. "You're not dirty, Jimmy. Please do this for me."

Jimmy held still as Eli stroked his cock. His eyes burned from his refusal to blink. Eli's lips parted on a gasp and his hips left the bed. Their erections slid across one another, creating the most delicious friction. Everything melted away except the gorgeous man beneath him. No one had ever made love to Jimmy before. Eli was now. It was beautiful.

Without thought, Jimmy rocked against Eli, allowing the friction between them to drag them closer to the edge. "You're so sexy," Jimmy praised. "And I'm so goddamn lucky."

"Please?" Eli begged, proving this wasn't enough.

Reaching between them, Jimmy palmed their cocks. With a pivot of his hips, he rocked into the touch, taking Eli with him. "So beautiful," Jimmy breathed. As always when Jimmy was with Eli, time didn't slip away. He'd never been more present for anything in his life. Sobriety had its perks. This was one thing he'd been missing. But then again, he'd never had this with anyone else.

Jimmy stared down at Eli, refusing to look away. White teeth sank into Eli's bottom lip, as if he bit back his moans.

"Don't," Jimmy begged. "Let me hear your pleasure."

Eli didn't give in right away. Jimmy slowed his pace but increased the pressure. A gasp escaped Eli. The man's every reaction fed Jimmy's. He held his orgasm at bay with sheer willpower. This man had Jimmy tied up in knots. Jimmy's name left Eli's lips on a soft moan.

"Damn, Eli. I want to be inside you. Your tight heat squeezing my dick gets me so high. I want you milking me."

As if Jimmy's words pushed Eli over the edge, hot cum coated Jimmy's fist. The sensation of Eli's cock jumping against his, mixed with the sensation of Eli's semen lubricating his strokes stole Jimmy's orgasm before he was ready give it. He'd meant every word. Jimmy needed Eli's ass squeezing him. Before he let Eli sleep again, he would get his way.

*

A loud shout pulled Eli from his sleep. Jimmy fought his way out from underneath the blankets. He tossed his legs over the edge of the bed before setting his elbows on his knees and cupping his head between his hands. Eli stared at the man's heaving back in silence. The urge to comfort him was crippling, but he knew in his heart he shouldn't touch Jimmy yet. He recognized he was dealing with the demons and not Jimmy at the moment. Instead of wrapping his arms around Jimmy and taking the pain into himself, as he wanted, Eli handled it the way he always did. He joined Jimmy in Hell.

"I had a brother. His name was Mark."

Jimmy's head shot up, but he didn't turn. Eli knew he had the man's attention.

"Before he died, he would hide me under his bed when our dad started in on us for the night. He would shove clothes, book, and whatever he could find under there with me so I'd be completely hidden from sight. When Dad would come looking for a fight, Mark always got it twice as bad because he wouldn't tell where he'd hidden me. No matter what Dad did to him, Mark never broke. He never told." Eli swallowed, wondering if he could do this. His gaze moved over Jimmy's back. The light gleaming across his sweat-soaked skin made the brand marring him stand out even more. Eli would do anything for Jimmy—even this.

189

"One day," Eli continued, "he got suspended from school for fighting. We both knew when Dad got home it would be bad. Mark had this look in his eyes—like I imagine someone would if they caught a glimpse of hell and couldn't unsee it." *The same way Jimmy looked sometimes*, Eli thought before pushing the idea from his mind. "Anyhow, he headed for our parents' bedroom. As he passed me, he gave me this look—like an apology. I couldn't move. My feet sort of glued to the carpet. I wanted to hide him the way he always hid me." Eli shook his head at the memory. "In all my life, I've never felt more useless. He opened their bedside table. I remember thinking he would be in twice as much trouble if he got caught in their room. He took out dad's gun and blew his brains out. Right there. No hesitation or looking back." Eli couldn't breathe. His chest rose and fell as he fought for air. It wouldn't come.

Without a word, Jimmy climbed back into bed and wrapped himself around Eli as if he could physically protect Eli from the past. "He left me alone," Eli said against Jimmy's chest. "Don't go away too, okay? I don't want to be alone again."

"Never," Jimmy said, sounding strong. Eli held him tighter. "I don't want you reliving nightmares for me. Tell me a good story instead."

At Jimmy's demand, Eli blushed. He could only think of one. It was something he'd never intended to confess, but desperate times... "About a year ago, I didn't have all the money together yet to pay you back. Still, I wanted to see you again. I showed up at the bar."

Jimmy lifted his head. "What? I never saw you."

The heat in Eli's cheeks increased. "I know."

A smile exploded across Jimmy's face. "A blush? Hmmm. I must know."

Eli buried his face against Jimmy's chest, refusing to look at him as he continued. "I waited for you outside the back door of the bar. You know, by the dumpster where you found me. When you finally came outside, you weren't alone. I started to leave, but you stopped right by the door. I couldn't get away without you seeing me."

"Wait," Jimmy said, bringing Eli's horror to an end. "The person I was with, what did they look like?"

Eli didn't have to think about it. The image was seared into his brain. "He was blond. His hair was a bit curly and he was taller than me but not by much."

"Oh my god," Jimmy breathed, sounding mortified and letting Eli know he remembered. Eli had watched as the blond had dropped to his knees and taken Jimmy's cock between his lips. As much as Eli had wanted to look away, he'd been incapable of tearing his gaze from the act taking place in that back alley. "Guess you got quite the show that night."

Eli pulled on some bravery he didn't know he possessed and met Jimmy's stare. "From the first night we met, I've wanted you. Maybe it wasn't me on my knees, but watching you with someone else still fed that desire to have you. My whole life, I've wanted things I couldn't have. You're the first dream I've ever had come true. I'll relive as many horror stories as I need to until the day comes we've gathered more happy memories than bad." Eli cupped Jimmy's jaw, needing every connection. "I'm with you, baby. Wherever you go."

Jimmy turned his head and pressed his lips to Eli's palm. As Eli looked on, his eyes fell closed. An unnamed emotion swelled in Eli's chest. A dimple appeared in Jimmy's cheek. The pressure in Eli's chest increased.

"Let's make a memory right now," Jimmy said, taking Eli by the hand.

"Okay."

At his agreement, Jimmy leapt from the bed. Eli enjoyed the vision he presented. The man wore only his underwear. He looked sexy as hell. Jimmy dug through his pants, coming out with his phone. He played with the device until music filled the tiny apartment. The smile stretching Eli's lips slipped away when Jimmy set the phone aside and pulled Eli to his feet.

"Nobody's watching," Jimmy said, making Eli wonder if he looked as horrified as he felt. Jimmy hauled Eli close and spun. A chuckle escaped him even as mortification overtook him. He'd never danced before in his life. The beat was fast, adding to his discomfort. Jimmy's smile had him willing to do anything to keep him that way. Laughter rose in Eli's throat as Jimmy made a show of shaking his ass. He tried keeping up without much luck. Not that Eli could stop laughing long enough to let the music guide him. The song ended. A slow song came on behind it. Jimmy slid in close. Eli's eyes fell closed as their skin met. His feet moved without his permission, matching Jimmy's steps. Jimmy buried his face against Eli's throat. Chill bumps rose on Eli's skin as Jimmy sang each loving word. His lips brushed

Eli's skin with every syllable.

A thought struck Eli. Just as Eli had been willing to travel to hell to get Jimmy, Jimmy was equally willing to create a heaven for Eli to follow. If he'd had a single doubt about moving in with Jimmy, it disappeared at the realization. This man was too damn amazing for words. Even if he ended up back on the streets, it would be worth every damn minute.

Chapter 8

For four solid months, Eli drove Jimmy's truck to and from work. That was, if Jimmy didn't take him and pick him up. Life still felt surreal. Maybe it was stupid, but Eli was still waiting for the other shoe to drop. He'd always heard that secrets destroyed relationships. It seemed they had them in droves. Jimmy never spoke of anything remotely related to his past. Most of the time, Eli didn't want to know—most of the time. A majority of the time, he didn't think it was important. Other times, he wondered if their pasts would float to the surface and destroy them. Something so ugly could only cause harm. There were moments when Eli would be on the verge of asking. Then he would look at Jimmy, and the words would die on his lips. One glance into Jimmy's eyes and Eli no longer cared what ate away at the man's soul. Instead, Eli vowed he'd always be the man's healing balm. His ghost exterminator. The man's dreamcatcher.

Tonight had been Eli's final night at Hollow Edge. Even now he still wasn't sure how he'd let Jimmy talk him into quitting. It was as if he couldn't stop handing Jimmy all the cards, giving the man the power to crush him in every way. The thing was—Eli didn't believe for a single second Jimmy would ever harm him. They were a team. That was why Eli had let Jimmy convince him to take a position with the bar. Eli would now be in charge of payroll and keeping the books. It was a damn good job for a man who only had a GED. Of course, Eli didn't lie to himself. He knew if they weren't together, Eli never would've been offered such a position.

At first, Eli had staunchly refused.

When Eli had gone to work the next day, he'd thought the whole thing over. He'd searched his heart. What Eli found shocked him. When it came to Jimmy, Eli trusted the man with everything he had. He knew beyond a doubt that he could put his future in Jimmy's hands, and no matter what happened between them, Jimmy wouldn't let anything happen to him. Once that thought settled in, his decision had been an easy one.

The house came into view. A flutter flared to life in Eli's gut. Although Eli knew the excitement would eventually fade into something more comfortable, it hadn't happened yet. He couldn't wait to see Jimmy. A strange car sat parked out front. Eli searched his mind for any hint of recognition and came up empty. As Eli pulled into the garage, he found himself hoping someone had broken down.

Otherwise, there was a stranger inside.

*

Jimmy kept one eye glued on the clock. Eli would be home any minute. He had to get Tyler out of there. The alarm chirped on the garage door, letting him know it was too late. Jimmy stared at the door—waiting. Tyler went on and on about counseling and moving forward with a lawsuit Jimmy wanted no part in. All Jimmy heard was "blah-blah" while his brain shifted into panic mode. What would he tell Eli? He'd never mentioned Tyler. In fact, he'd never mentioned a million details about his life.

The back door opened. Those green eyes—the ones that made Jimmy's heart race—made an appearance. In spite of his horrible position, Jimmy smiled at the sight of his man coming home to him. He hoped it wasn't for the last time.

"Hey, baby. How was work?"

Tyler turned in his seat.

Jimmy ignored him.

Eli's lips turned up in the corners, as if happy to see him, before his smile melted away as his gaze slid Tyler's way. "Hello." Damn. Eli sounded wary.

Tyler came to his feet.

Jimmy did too. He stepped around Tyler, incapable of letting the man touch Eli, tainting him with Jimmy's past. Before Tyler could introduce himself, Jimmy pressed a quick kiss to Eli's lips.

"Sorry I didn't warn you we had company. I wasn't expecting any." Jimmy didn't bother hiding his aggravation over that last point.

"It's okay," Eli said, attempting to peer over Jimmy's shoulder. "Do I get to meet our company or are we going to stand here awkwardly all day long?"

Since it couldn't be avoided, Jimmy tucked Eli beneath his arm, making it obvious he didn't want Tyler touching Eli. "Eli, this is Tyler. Tyler, this is Eli." Jimmy purposely didn't expound on the introduction.

Obviously reading Jimmy's body language, Tyler didn't try to shake Eli's hand. "It's nice to meet you, Eli."

Eli nodded. Jimmy felt like shit. He knew Eli hated meeting new people, and he made things worse by not divulging who Tyler was. If Jimmy came home to a strange man in their house, there would be hell to pay and demands made. Eli wasn't like that. He was too sweet for confrontation.

Eli cast a glance around the kitchen. "I

hope you just got here, since it doesn't look like Jimmy has offered you anything to drink."

Tyler's smile turned genuine. Dimples and all. "Not too long, no."

Eli's shoulders relaxed. "Would you like something to drink?"

"Sure. Water is fine."

With a nod, Eli moved to the refrigerator. Jimmy warned Tyler with his gaze to watch himself. Tyler turned his back on Jimmy and sat, letting him know this visit could go either way.

"Damn," Eli muttered under his breath. "There's no more bottled water."

"From the tap is fine," Tyler said over his shoulder, letting them know he'd heard. He also sounded a hell of a lot nicer now than he had before Eli's arrival.

Jimmy couldn't look away from Eli's face. He needed to know his man was okay. Eli curled his nose at Tyler's words. It was adorable, and went a long way at easing the pressure building in Jimmy's chest.

"One tap water coming up." Eli's gaze locked on Jimmy. "Do you want anything, baby?"

To drink his bar. The whole thing. After that, he wanted to take Eli to bed and never leave. "I should be asking you. You're the one who just got home. As a matter of fact," Jimmy said, grabbing a glass from the cabinet. "Go change or whatever. I got this."

Eli cast a glance Tyler's way. "Are you sure? Is that rude?"

Sometimes, Eli made everything clean again with his innocent worries. Jimmy's throat swelled. Tyler shouldn't be here, poisoning their home. "It's not rude. Promise," Jimmy added when Eli didn't look convinced.

With a nod, Eli headed down the hall. Jimmy's gaze followed Eli's every move until their bedroom door closed behind him. The moment he was out of sight, Jimmy slammed the glass down in front of Tyler.

"Here's your fucking water."

Tyler's smirk might've been comical under different circumstances. With Eli right down the hall, and Tyler on the verge of ruining Jimmy's shot at a normal life, there was nothing funny about any of this.

"This is an interesting new development in your life."

Jimmy refused the bait.

"How old is he? He looks young."

Biting back a growl, Jimmy spoke through clenched teeth. "Twenty-one, you nosey bastard. I'm not like—" Jimmy bit off his words, incapable of finishing.

Tyler sighed. "Even after all these years, you still can't even say his name." Tyler's face softened. "I know you're not like him. I was simply making conversation." Tyler's gaze flickered over Jimmy's shoulder a half second before Eli's hands landed on Jimmy's shoulders. His muscles relaxed at the contact. Eli's touch was like a healing balm.

"I hate to seem rude, but I haven't eaten at all today."

Jimmy snagged one of Eli's hands and brought it to his mouth. "Don't worry over it, baby," he soothed against the man's skin. "I don't want you going hungry."

Tyler's smile turned bright once more as he glanced Eli's way—the smarmy bastard. "Please act as if I'm not here and do whatever you need."

With a final squeeze of Jimmy's fingers, Eli pulled away and headed for the stove. With Eli still in earshot, he didn't know how to get rid of Tyler. The man couldn't stay. Every muscle in Jimmy's body was on the verge of snapping. His mind raced for something to say before Tyler opened his mouth and ruined Jimmy's life.

"Did you get what you came for?"

Pans clanged together. Tyler's smile took on a sinister edge, as if he knew he had Jimmy on the ropes with Eli there and planned to exploit his power.

"No."

Jimmy's fear fled. In its place sat a

rage he hadn't experienced in years. "That's too bad." Even Jimmy heard the growl in his tone.

Eli froze, frying pan in hand. He eyed Jimmy. Worry etched his features.

Jimmy sat forward, focusing his fury on Tyler. "You should go."

Tyler didn't budge. "I never put you out, even though there were many times when you deserved it. Besides," Tyler added. "I haven't finished my water."

"Don't try to guilt trip me," Jimmy said, his voice rising. "This situation isn't the same."

"No. It isn't," Tyler said, raising his voice to top Jimmy's. "You were Satan's spawn, while I'm sitting here drinking some goddamn water. That's not the same at all." With every word Tyler spoke, his voice got louder until he was yelling at the top of his lungs. He pushed the glass aside and came to his feet. Jimmy did the same until they were nose-to-nose across the table. Tyler wasn't finished. "In fact, while I graciously endured—"

Jimmy snorted. "Graciously, my ass," Jimmy interrupted.

Tyler ignored him, only yelling louder. "While I *graciously*," he repeated, "endured all your goddamn bullshit, you can't even listen to me for five fucking minutes when I have your best interests at heart. You've always had issues..."

"I think you should go."

"...real fucking fucked in the head problems, but this is some—"

A loud crash had their heads snapping around in Eli's direction. He stood frozen, with his arm still extended from where he smashed out the kitchen window with the frying pan. Jimmy didn't know how to react. Eli's eyes—fuck. He was freaking out on the inside. Jimmy could see it happening. It was a silent panic attack, and it was the scariest thing Jimmy had seen in years. Judging by Tyler's expression, he didn't know what to do either.

"Baby," Jimmy said almost too quiet to hear, hoping to break the spell. Eli blinked. Otherwise, he didn't move at all. It was like witnessing the calm before the storm. Jimmy's muscles tensed, expecting anything.

Eli focused on Tyler. "You were asked to leave." His voice was soft and deadly. Jimmy feared for Tyler's life.

Jimmy took a step in Eli's direction, half expecting to get reamed by a frying pan. To his surprise, Eli set the pan aside before stepping around them and heading down the hall. Their bedroom door snapped closed behind him.

"You should've told me," Tyler said with regret tinging his words and pulling Jimmy's gaze away from the closed door. "I never would've yelled had I known."

Pain lodged in Jimmy's throat. He was the one who should've known better. He should've thrown Tyler in the street long before Eli came home. That didn't cool his temper. He met the gaze of the man who'd given him a home when he'd been a fucked up and half-wild teenager no one else wanted. Sadness washed over him.

"I should've told you what? This is his home, not yours. You should've known only someone broken could care about me, and behaved accordingly. Goddamn, Tyler," Jimmy said, shaking his head. He didn't know what to say, so he walked away and went after Eli. Tyler could stay or go. Jimmy no longer cared. Eli needed him.

He half expected the door to be locked. The knob turned easily beneath his hand. What he found inside their room almost made him wish the door had been locked. Eli was packing his things.

"Is this some fall version of spring cleaning?"

Eli didn't respond.

"Because I know you're not leaving me," he added when Eli didn't stop.

"It's better this way," Eli said, shoving his clothes in an overnight bag. "Eventually, you'll get sick of having a crazy person living with you."

Jimmy sighed. "Baby, I had a crazy person living with me before you moved in, and you're not insane."

Eli finally looked at him. His eyes were still every bit as wild as they'd been in the kitchen. "I busted out the window. It's like I couldn't stop it from happening. It was the window or Tyler's head."

"He likely wouldn't have noticed," Jimmy said, trying to hang on to a calm tone. "Tyler's pretty damn hardheaded."

Eli covered his face, gulping for air. "Jesus. I don't know what's going on."

This was Jimmy's fault. He'd left Eli in the dark about so many damn things. With a tug, he pulled Eli into his arms. "Come here," Jimmy said, urging Eli onto the bed before climbing on top of him. He had a dual purpose. Not only did Jimmy need to hold Eli, he couldn't let the man get away. No way in hell would he let Eli leave him. As he hovered above Eli, elbows braced on either side of the man's head while trying to decide what to do, his hair fell forward, surrounding them. Cutting them off from the world.

"If I bust out two windows, would you feel better?"

Eli stared at him in silence, but some of the fire left his eyes.

"Is that a no?" Jimmy asked. "What about three? I could get one in every room of the house," Jimmy said, warming up to the idea. He could stand some anger release.

"Why aren't you mad at me?"

At Eli's question, a pain hit Jimmy in the chest. "Because you were standing up for me, first off. I'd rather have you in my corner than anyone else on the planet. You're badass," Jimmy said, meaning it.

One corner of Eli's mouth lifted. Some of the pressure in Jimmy's chest eased.

Unexpectedly, Jimmy's eyes stung. "I guess you know by now, my life hasn't been good."

Eli held his gaze, but he didn't answer.

"If I tell you about Tyler, could you live without knowing the rest?"

"You don't even have to tell me about Tyler, if you don't want," Eli said without missing a beat.

"Yes, I do," Jimmy argued. Eli had no clue how bare minimum the story of Tyler would be. "For many years, he was a police detective for the Orange County Police department. Of course, when I met him, he had just gotten hired as a beat cop. I was fourteen and no one else would take me. In hindsight, I realize he wasn't much older than me." Jimmy snorted. "He was such a hardass, he seemed older. That's why he yells," Jimmy explained. "Even though I'm grown, and we're nearly the same age, he still sees me as that fourteen-year-old kid he took in." Jimmy swallowed, hoping Eli would accept his half-ass explanation. "Seeing him reminds me of things I want to forget. He wants me to do something that will dredge up my past, and I can't go down that path again."

The understanding in Eli's gaze made Jimmy's throat burn. "Eli," Jimmy whispered. "You can't leave me. Nobody else understands and keeps me sane. I can't lose you without losing me too."

"I love moments like these."

Eli's statement seemed at such odds with the day, he had to know. "Moments like what?"

Eli ran his fingers through Jimmy's hair, keeping it fanned out around them. "When your hair falls around us, creating our own little haven. It's like we're alone in the world and nothing can touch us."

Jimmy's lungs ceased working. All the times he'd felt the same, he hadn't been alone. "I love you."

At Jimmy's claim, Eli stopped playing with his hair and focused on Jimmy. "What?"

Jimmy didn't look away. Not only had he never uttered those words to anyone, he'd never heard them from anyone who didn't have a sick purpose for saying them. "I love you," Jimmy repeated, because it was true, and Eli deserved to hear it. "You're my conscience and my sanity. My home. You can't leave me, okay?"

"Okay," Eli said sounding sweet. "Jimmy."

"Yeah."

"I love you too."

It was every bit as amazing as he always feared it would be. Hearing those words on Eli's lips, knowing he meant them, it was an instant addiction. The high was unlike anything he'd ever experienced. He wanted to hear them again and again.

"I love you," Jimmy said, needing the words right now.

"I love you too."

Jimmy's eyes fell closed. It was the closest to crying he'd been since he was a child. Warm lips touched his. Everything Eli did, he did in the sweetest way possible. He was clean.

Their lips clung.

"Make love to me," Eli pled. "Take away this sickness sitting in my gut."

Jimmy sat back on his heels and pulled his shirt over his head. The small distance between them was too much. He wanted their haven back. In hopes of hurrying things along, he left the bed and pulled Eli to his feet. As he divested Eli of his clothes, Jimmy realized Eli wasn't interested in sex. The man wasn't even hard. What Eli sought was intimacy. Jimmy would give him anything he needed.

Once they were nude, Jimmy pulled the covers back, and urged Eli onto the bed. Jimmy followed him down. He pulled the covers over them as he settled between Eli's thighs once more. Their bodies pressed against each other. Eli cradled Jimmy's weight. They were the perfect fit. He kissed Eli gently, allowing his lips to linger before seeking entry. Their tongues met briefly before retreating once more.

Neither one sought anything beyond the other's company. Whispered words of love passed between them each time they pulled away before going back for more.

The sun dipped low in the sky, casting a shadow upon the room. They held each other, kissing and exchanging touches. Jimmy's heart had never been fuller. He was at peace. Quiet filled his mind like he'd never experienced before. He didn't need anything. Not alcohol or rage. He also didn't miss a moment of Eli—the brush of Eli's inner thighs against his hips. The way Eli's feet brushed his. All of Eli's broken pieces fit seamlessly into Jimmy's cracked shell. Together, they created one perfect and beautiful soul. Until sleep pulled him under, Jimmy enjoyed every kiss and touch from this man who completed him.

*

Jimmy's long lashes cast a shadow upon his cheeks. Eli wanted to watch the man sleep all night. His sexy lips were swollen from Eli's kisses. No matter how much time passed, Eli still had a hard time believing this gorgeous man belonged to him. Now Jimmy had said he loved him. Eli's heart swelled with happiness and pride. In spite of all Eli's flaws, Jimmy loved him. No one had ever been as lucky as Eli felt in that moment.

His stomach growled, reminding Eli he hadn't eaten. As much as he didn't want to leave their bed, Eli knew there would be no sleeping until he got something to eat. Not to mention, he needed to do something about their kitchen window. Jimmy was sleeping now, but it wouldn't be long before he'd be up, worrying over their home being unsecured.

Eli eased from the bed, doing his best

not to wake Jimmy. When Jimmy didn't stir, Eli quickly pulled on his clothes before sneaking from the room. The scent of coffee brewing hit Eli the instant he opened the bedroom door. He found Tyler sitting at the kitchen table, reading a book with the coffee pot at his elbow. He glanced up as Eli shuffled into the kitchen.

"You're still here."

Tyler nodded. "I couldn't leave without apologizing. Plus, I had to wait on the guys to show up and replace the window."

Eli's gaze shot to the window. The mess was gone and the glass was pristine, as if nothing happened. "You had the window replaced," Eli said—like he couldn't stop pointing out the obvious.

"It was the least I could do. Like I said, I owe you an apology. For almost twenty years, I've worked as part of a task force for endangered and exploited children. I had no business coming into your home and behaving the way I did. If anyone should know better, it's me."

That was just fantastic. Tyler thought he was a head case. He was, but still. "What are you reading?"

Tyler flipped the book over at Eli's question. "I have no idea. Something I found on the shelf." He focused on Eli. "Seriously, who doesn't own a TV?"

"Us," Eli answered without an ounce of shame. "I don't like the noise and Jimmy works all the time. Or at least, he used to."

Tyler nodded. "I see."

Eli had no idea what Tyler saw, but he thought it might be time to change the subject. "Jimmy tells me you took him in when no one else was willing."

"You said you were hungry earlier," Tyler said, ignoring Eli's statement. "Since I'm the reason you missed dinner, I picked you up something. It's in the microwave."

Eli moved to the microwave and looked inside. A plate of chicken, mashed potatoes, and biscuits sat waiting for him. It was cool to the touch. Eli started the device and watched as the plate turned, warming the food. He didn't know what to do with his hands. Even though he knew Tyler wasn't watching him, Eli felt on display—exposed.

"In the twenty years I've known Jimmy," Tyler said while still looking at the book and breaking the silence, "I've never seen him when he wasn't either enraged or drunk. Until today."

"He seemed pretty angry to me earlier."

Tyler chuckled at Eli's observation. It

was a low and comforting sound. It had Eli taking a closer look at the man. His brown hair curled at the ends and brushed his neck. It looked soft. In fact, the man seemed softer than Eli expected.

"That wasn't angry Jimmy. That was slightly-put-out Jimmy."

The microwave beeped, pulling Eli's attention its way. He checked the chicken again. Finding it warm, he grabbed the plate and joined Tyler at the table.

"Thank you for the food."

Tyler glanced up from the book, focusing on Eli with the lightest gray eyes Eli had ever seen. Instead of acknowledging his thanks, Tyler went back to staring at the book before saying anything else. Eli appreciated it. He didn't like eating in front of strangers. It was as if Tyler had read the textbook on dealing with Eli and followed the instructions.

"Almost four years ago, I got a call from a friend of mine, saying Jimmy's name had popped up in the system. He'd been arrested on his second DUI. I waited for close to a month before dropping in to check on him, because I knew he wouldn't appreciate it."

Eli ate and listened. He assumed this story had a point. All he needed was to wait for it. Tyler turned the page as if he was still reading even as he spoke.

"When I got here, he was drunk as usual, but he was also eerily clearheaded. For once, he didn't rage against my presence. He asked if I knew anyone on the local endangered children's task force. I said yeah. Me. I'd decided with this being his second DUI, I needed to move closer and keep an eye on things. So I transferred." Tyler shook his head.

"Instead of being angry, as I expected, he told me an interesting story. Seems he tried helping out some homeless kid, and the boy robbed him before disappearing. I'd never seen him care about anyone other than himself. I didn't hesitate agreeing to keep an eye out for the kid."

Tyler looked up again. Eli kept his face carefully blank. "I never did find him. Of course, I didn't have much to go on besides a vague description and a first name." Eli didn't breathe again until Tyler went back to staring at the inside of his book. "Maybe I'm wrong to keep coming here."

Even though Tyler wasn't that much older than Jimmy, Eli thought he sounded the way a parent should. He hadn't given up on Jimmy. That said a lot about him.

"Maybe you should try coming around without wanting anything from him.

Jimmy isn't a project. He's a person. He doesn't need you to try to fix him." Since Tyler wasn't arguing and seemed genuinely interested in Eli's opinion, Eli didn't stop. "No amount of yelling or bullying will make someone else's demons go away when they live in their head."

"You seem to be doing something right. He loves you."

Heat flooded Eli's cheeks.

Tyler smiled. It was the kindest smile Eli had ever seen. He wasn't sure what Tyler's job entailed, but Eli imagined children found him comforting, even at their lowest.

"He saved me," Jimmy said, startling Eli. He hadn't heard the bedroom door open. Jimmy's arms encircled him from behind a half second before his lips landed on the side of Eli's neck. Eli's eyes fell closed.

"We saved each other," Eli whispered for Jimmy's ears alone. When his eyes opened, he found Tyler staring at him as if trying to solve a puzzle.

"What have the two of you been doing while I was sleeping?"

"Tyler bought me dinner and replaced the window," Eli said, hoping to soften Jimmy. He didn't think he could handle any more yelling today.

Jimmy eyed his plate. "It doesn't look like you've eaten anything, but you never do." He stole a piece of Eli's chicken. Jimmy's lips touched Eli's shoulder as if that made up for taking his food before claiming the seat at Eli's side.

"Eli says you're no longer working yourself to death," Tyler said as soon as Jimmy was seated. Eli didn't think he'd used those exact words, but it also didn't matter.

Jimmy shrugged. "The club in Nashville has always run itself. I just like hanging out there. Now, I'm thinking of selling it."

That was the first Eli had heard of Jimmy selling anything.

"My bar here has good management, so I'm not really needed there. Not to mention, it's easier not to drink if I'm not sitting there smelling alcohol all day."

"What have you been doing with all your extra time? Looks like you've put on some more muscle since the last time I saw you."

Eli hid his smile. He was grateful Tyler hadn't remarked on Jimmy not drinking. The man could backslide any day. Eli would still love him, but he wanted Jimmy to succeed.

"I've been forcing Eli to come to the gym with me."

Jimmy's statement pulled a surprised bark of laughter from Eli. "He has, but I just go to watch."

"Don't let him lie to you," Jimmy said, sounding happy. "He always takes a book with him. I doubt he sees anything at all."

"I watch your matches," Eli shot back in mock outrage.

"So you're still fighting?" Tyler asked. "How's that going?"

Eli watched the pair chatting about nothing. Jimmy looked more relaxed than he had in a long time while in anyone's company other than his. Hope grew in Eli's chest. Jimmy needed more people in his life who loved him. Maybe Tyler hadn't been showing it, but the man did care. The world seemed a little brighter than it had a few hours earlier—like there could be a real future for them.

Chapter 9

"You want to hit the gym with me?"

Eli glanced down at himself. "Am I getting fat?"

Jimmy scoffed. "No. I have a sparring match scheduled. You're going to cheer me on." He hesitated before adding, "You can take your book too, of course."

Jimmy hadn't needed to tack on that bit. Eli was happy to go anywhere Jimmy wanted. "Sounds great." As Eli came to his feet, Jimmy rushed to help. It was a ploy. He pulled Eli into his arms and stole a kiss. Not that he'd needed to steal anything. That shit was free. Eli would take any of Jimmy's touches any way he could get them. Jimmy's thin workout shorts did nothing to hide the erection bumping Eli's stomach. Eli licked Jimmy's bottom lip and pulled away long enough to toss his book on the couch before going back for more. His fingers automatically went for the string of Jimmy's shorts.

"How much time do you have?" Eli asked against Jimmy's mouth. He savored the way Jimmy's hands moved down the length of his body, grabbing Eli's ass and pulling him closer.

"I'll make time for anything you want."

Eli matched Jimmy's stroke of tongue on tongue before pulling away and kissing the man's throat. He hadn't shaved in a few days. Eli savored the way the rough bristles scraped across his lips. Jimmy tilted his head back, surrendering to Eli. He loved that shit. Craved the control Jimmy always gave him. It was an illusion. Jimmy could walk away at any time, and there'd be nothing Eli could do, but he never did. He always gave Eli license to do as he pleased. Now was no different and Eli reveled in it.

He set Jimmy's erection free and stroked him. "I want you screaming my name," he said against Jimmy's throat before slipping to his knees. Jimmy tried snagging him under his arms and pulling back to his feet. Eli was having none of it.

"You don't have to do this."

Eli stared up the line of Jimmy's body. "Yes. I do." While holding the man's stare, Eli leaned in and placed a light kiss to his crown. He swore Jimmy's eyes darkened. Maybe Jimmy didn't need this in his life, but he liked it. Eli needed to be whole for Jimmy. This was the first step. Eli's tongue shot out, stroking the spot he'd kissed.

"Not like this," Jimmy said, joining Eli on the floor. "If you're determined to do this, I won't have you on your knees at my feet. That's not how life with me works." Eli nodded, even though he wasn't sure he cared. He'd gladly set the world at Jimmy's feet if he could. His dick throbbed with need. Jimmy was so fucking sexy. Eli wanted to make him happy. For a moment, Jimmy's lips brushed Eli's, before he melted to the floor, taking Eli with him. He pushed at Eli's shorts. "Take these off. We'll do this together."

The promise of pleasure had Eli rushing to comply. The instant he was nude, Jimmy snagged Eli's thigh and urged him to straddle Jimmy's face. Damn. It was good. The heat of Jimmy's tongue and the pull of his mouth had Eli's fears falling away. Taking Jimmy's cock between his lips, Eli mimicked the man's motions. It took all his willpower to focus on his task. Even with nothing to compare him to, Eli recognized Jimmy had talent. The man could pull off tricks everyone dreamed about.

The way Eli's nerve endings danced and sang held Eli's brain captive. Saliva dripped from Eli's lips, coating Jimmy's dick and stomach. If there was an ounce of fear or disgust inside Eli, he couldn't find it. All he knew was pleasure and power because it was Jimmy. Nothing wrong happened between them. They were each other's safe zone.

Jimmy moaned around Eli's cock. The sound vibrated up Eli's shaft, drawing his balls tight. His throat burned, making Eli realize how deep he'd been taking Jimmy. Without thought, Eli's hips moved. He openly fucked Jimmy's mouth. The sounds Jimmy made and the way he fingered Eli's ass had Eli hanging on by a thread. Things always escalated so quickly between them. Only moments earlier, he'd been peacefully reading. Now, Jimmy's cum filled his mouth and waves of pleasure pulsed through Eli. He'd started this with no clue where it would lead. Eli hadn't expected Jimmy to taste delicious.

Damn. He couldn't stop licking the man's dick, hunting for more of his salt. The way Jimmy pled for Eli and chanted his name added fuel to the fire. This was Heaven. Jimmy was his place in the world. Sometimes the knowledge threatened to move him to tears. Other people—normal people—might not have lived their nightmare, but those people also would never know their bliss. Love was everything.

* * *

"You're late," Ryan said with a definite bark to his tone.

238

"I apologize." Jimmy glanced over Ryan's shoulder and shook his head, mouthing, "I'm not sorry."

Eli bit back a laugh.

"Yeah, yeah," Ryan said, getting Jimmy back on track.

"Don't let him fool you," Logan said, appearing out of nowhere and claiming the seat next to Eli. "I made him late too."

Eli chuckled. He genuinely liked Logan, especially since he made Jimmy's life easier at the bar. "Where's Malik?"

"He's waiting for his turn," Logan answered, nodding toward where Malik stood off to the side at the edge of the mat. "He gets the winner next. What are you reading?" Logan asked, eyeing Eli's book.

Eli showed him the cover. "It's the new T.L. Crisp. Well, I suppose it's not that new

239

any longer, but I'm just now getting to it."

Logan toyed with the cover, flipping it open. "Is this the book you got in Atlanta?"

"Yeah. How did you know about Atlanta?"

"Jimmy talks about you nonstop," Logan said, making Eli's day. "I thought he got you an e-reader for Valentine's Day? I guess I should've realized—if he took you to a signing—you'd get an actual book."

Eli shook his head. "He did get me an e-reader. Before we left the house, he made me put it in his gym bag just in case things ran long today. I still have quite a way to go in this one," he said, flashing the book at Logan once more. "But Jimmy always goes overboard."

A sexy-sounding chuckle escaped Logan. If the man didn't already have more men than any one person should, Eli would have to hate him on principle alone. "He loves you. People always go overboard when their hearts are involved. He wants you to have the world."

Eli didn't know how to respond. When he didn't say anything, Logan looked away from the match and focused on him.

"I don't think I ever thanked you."

Against his will, Eli's face screwed up in confusion. "For what?"

Logan nodded toward the ring. "You changed him—for the better, of course. Jimmy, he keeps to himself and doesn't show anyone his heart. In spite of all that, I've always thought the world of him. Unfortunately, I also thought he'd kill himself before too long with all the drinking. Then you came along." Logan's gaze moved over Eli's face, as if searching for something. "I don't know what you did, but you saved him somehow."

Eli looked away. Logan's inspection was too much. Instead, he watched Jimmy and Ryan trying to best each other. Strands of Jimmy's hair came loose from his bun, falling into his face. They clung to his sweat. The muscles in Eli's stomach clenched. "He saved me." A smile touched Eli's lips. He could feel Logan watching him.

"Oh, look. Ryan won."

Personally, Eli thought Jimmy let him win, but Eli was loyal like that.

"It was nice chatting with you," Logan said, coming to his feet. "I'm gonna move closer. Watching Ryan and Malik, straining against each other, always makes me hot." Logan's smile had Eli biting back a sigh. It really was no wonder Logan snagged two men.

"I'd think you'd get to see that all the time at home." As the words left his lips, horror set in. It wasn't like him to say such things. "Oh my God. I don't know what happened right then."

Laughter shone bright in Logan's eyes, setting Eli at ease. "You're coming to think of me as your friend. I like this new naughty side of you. You should keep it up. We'll get along great." The heat in Eli's cheeks was more from Logan's praise than embarrassment.

Jimmy moved to join them. "Look at my two favorite people, laughing and—most likely—plotting my downfall. It warms my heart."

Logan snorted. Before the man could let whatever smartass retort he'd gather fly, Jimmy kissed Eli.

"Best get to my men," Logan said,

sounding overly loud and bright.

Jimmy chuckled against Eli's lips, pulling a smile from Eli. The happiness in Jimmy's eyes, as he pulled away, had Eli near to squirming in his seat. That elation was due to him. He'd done that. Somehow, Eli had made this amazing man happy, and he didn't want to ever stop.

"Are you okay to hang out a little longer?"

Eli nodded. "I'm good."

Jimmy eyed him. "Are you sure? I want to hit the weights for a bit before we go, but I could skip it."

"It's fine," Eli said, waving him away. "I've got my book."

Jimmy pressed another quick kiss to Eli's lips before snagging his gym bag off the floor. He set it in the seat Logan vacated. "Don't forget your e-reader is inside if you get bored."

A heavy sigh escaped Eli. "Baby, I'm good. Go. Do your thing." He held the book up, showing Jimmy he still had quite a way to go. "As far as I'm concerned, I'm on Zacron nine, trying to repair my ship."

Jimmy didn't laugh, as Eli had hoped. Instead, his gaze flashed with heat. "Once I finish up here, I'll take you on a trip to cloud nine."

"I like this plan." Even Eli heard the lust tinting his words.

Jimmy's mouth lifted in one corner. "I'll hurry."

With a final kiss, Jimmy was off. Eli tried hard to concentrate on his book. The words kept blurring. The phantom flavor of Jimmy's cock kept filling Eli's mouth. Damn. He was an addict. Eli couldn't wait to have Jimmy alone again.

"Hey."

Eli glanced up from his book, expecting one of Logan's men... or Satan. Anyone other than Jace. The man was so pretty. It was sickening. His eyes were sweet and his lips were perfect.

"Hi."

Jace waved at the chair next to Eli. "Do you mind if I join you?"

Eli glanced over at Jimmy's bag. Did he want to chat with Jace? No, but it seemed it was happening regardless of his feelings. Eli moved the bag. "Sure." Even to his ears, Eli didn't sound sure at all.

"We haven't officially met. I'm Jace Preston," Jace said, holding out his hand.

Eli closed his book, holding his place with one finger before shaking Jace's hand.

"Eli Everett."

"No offense, but you look really young." Jace smiled as he said the words, as if attempting to take the sting from them.

Some form of fuck-it-all rose in Eli's chest. "Since I was homeless and starving for some pivotal years of my life, I'm not surprised you think so. Malnutrition can fuck you up."

Jace flushed.

Eli fought the urge not to roll his eyes. He couldn't care less if Jace was embarrassed.

"That explains a lot. Jimmy's always been a sucker for hopeless cases." Eli jerked back, as if Jace had slapped him. Jace blinked. Eli swore he could see the man scrambling for more to say. He cleared his throat. "Wow. Contrary to how that sounded, I did hear myself right then, and that's not what I meant. You have beautiful eyes and seem nice. I didn't mean to imply Jimmy only wants you because of his past."

Hell would freeze before Eli asked. "What are you talking about?" Fuck. Had aliens hijacked his mind? Jace was back to blinking, as if sending out Morse code for help. Eli held his stare—waiting.

Jace cast a desperate glance around the room, as if searching for anything else to talk about. His gaze landed on the book in Eli's lap. "What are you reading?"

Eli automatically held out his book for Jace to see, even as his mind raced for answers. This man knew why Jimmy was the way he was, and Eli needed that info. "It's a sci-fi horror novel," Eli answered absently, scrambling for a way to convince Jace to tell him everything he needed to know.

"Do you like true crime novels as well?"

Eli had never wanted to shake some answers out of anyone as badly in his life as he did right then. Still, he nodded. "If it's well-written."

Jace nodded and chewed on his bottom lip, as if trying to decide if he should say something. He turned inside himself for a moment before focusing on Eli once more. One way or the other, the man had decided. "You should check out a book called *A Boy Forgotten* by Garrison Levy. You might find it... enlightening."

"Okay."

Jace smiled at Eli's agreement. "It was nice meeting you, Eli. Maybe say hi next time you're around."

Eli dipped his chin, incapable of agreeing. Lord, he hoped there wouldn't be a next time, even as he knew that was an impossible dream. As Jace pulled his shirt over his head and climbed into the ring, Eli watched it happened. He didn't like always thinking the worst. Eli recognized it was an old survival mechanism. Nowadays, it was hard pushing past his habits to gauge people. Jace was sexy. No doubt, he had tons of men falling at his feet. People were watching him now with hunger in their stares. He didn't think Jace would do or say anything to simply spite Jimmy or him. The man wasn't a mean person. Maybe a little awkward, but Eli couldn't judge anyone on that front. The way he'd spoken about that book...

Eli unzipped Jimmy's bag. After a second of hunting, he found his e-reader and connected to the gym's Wi-Fi. Thanks to Jace giving him the name of the author as well as the title, Eli didn't have any trouble finding the book. The cover was somewhat disturbing. It was nothing more than one side of a child's face, staring out a nondescript window. Eli scrolled down to the blurb.

The unofficial story of Jimmy Stone. Sold in a drug deal at only eight years old, Jimmy was held captive for six years by a well-known serial pedophile.

Everything inside Eli froze with horror. His stomach churned. He couldn't read another word. The last name was different, but Eli felt it in his gut—this was his Jimmy. Tears pressed against the backs of his eyes. An invisible weight fell on his shoulders, stealing all the oxygen from the room. So many things suddenly made sense. Jimmy's reaction the morning after they slept together for the

251

first time. The drinking and the lights staying on all night. A thousand tiny details came together, revealing a horrible image. He'd known whatever nightmare lived inside Jimmy was worse than hell, but this... His heart hurt.

"My sexy baby right where I left him," Jimmy said, appearing over him and swooping in for a kiss.

Eli tried flipping the device over as their lips met, but he lost his grip. It slid to the floor, smacking the hard surface, sounding unnaturally loud to Eli's overwrought nerves.

Jimmy went down onto his haunches and scooped it up. He flipped the device over in his hands, inspecting it for damage. "It doesn't look—" Jimmy froze. His gaze fixed upon the screen. Time stopped. Eli didn't know what to do. Even the air seemed to hold its breath.

Eli broke beneath the strain. "I wasn't... Jace..." His hands lifted and fell back to his lap. He'd never felt more out of his depth.

Jimmy's gaze shifted back to Eli's face. He handed Eli the e-reader. "I guess you're wondering if it's really me."

Eli shook his head, fighting back tears. "I know it's you."

Jimmy blew out a sigh, causing the loose strands of hair around his face to fly out in waves. "In a way, I'm relieved. I've been searching for a way to tell you. It didn't seem fair that Jace knows when he means nothing to me. I talk too much when I'm drinking," Jimmy said, rubbing his palms on Eli's thighs in an absent motion and making Eli wonder which of them he was trying to comfort. "One night, the night I meet you, actually, he was screaming at me about how selfish I was because I wouldn't give up my addiction for him—to save our relationship." Jimmy smiled. It was frightening. Eli's lungs labored beneath the sight of it, but he didn't think Jimmy was really there at the moment. "I told him I couldn't be fixed, so he needed to stop trying. He kept pushing and so I told him everything." Jimmy's gaze sharpened, as if returning to the present. "I'm sorry."

Outrage boiled beneath Eli's skin, threatening to bring out his horrible temper. "Why are you sorry? Jace should be—"

Jimmy waved a dismissive hand, cutting him off. "No doubt he thought to save you the same heartache I caused him. Do you want to hear something funny?"

"There's something funny?" Eli asked, incapable of hiding the horror in his voice.

"Sure," Jimmy answered with a bright smile. "That night, I was too drunk and pissed off to hear anything Jace had to say. Since meeting you, I realize he was right. When the right one came along and I fell in love, I didn't want to drink anymore. Not that it's been easy, but you've been worth it." Eli was still too horrified by everything he'd learned to think clearly. It took him a minute to hear all the wonderful things Jimmy had said alongside the ugly facts. Before he could respond, Jimmy's smile fell, killing the words in his throat. He squeezed Eli's thighs. "Don't read it, okay? It would kill me if you looked at me differently."

"I won't," Eli promised. He didn't want to know.

Jimmy let his knees hit the floor between Eli's feet before moving closer. "I'll tell you how it ends, if you'd like?"

Eli couldn't draw a full breath. "You survived. That's all I need."

Jimmy shook his head. His gaze never wavered from Eli's as he encircled Eli's waist, as if scared he'd bolt. "I existed. That's not the same as surviving. I killed him." Jimmy said the words fast—like ripping off a bandage. By the set of Jimmy's jaw, Eli wondered if Jimmy expected Eli to reject him now.

"Good."

His features relaxed. With a quick nod, Jimmy acknowledged Eli's praise. "When I turned eighteen, I was awarded a settlement from the state. I changed my last name and moved here. In my youth, I thought I could run away—start over." A sad smile passed over his features. "It didn't take me long to realize I couldn't escape my mind." He paused. Eli wanted to say something—anything. Words failed him. He twisted at his fingers in his lap, feeling more useless than ever before. Jimmy continued, sparing him from thinking of something to say. "Before you ask, I've had counseling. I've had a lot of help, actually. It didn't work."

"I imagine it wouldn't."

Jimmy nodded. "The only thing that keeps me sane is knowing he's dead."

"It's helping me a lot at the moment too," Eli admitted. Although he still wanted to find the man's grave, dig him up, and kill him again.

An unexpected smile exploded across Jimmy's face. "I love you."

Because he couldn't take anymore, Eli leaned forward and set his forehead against Jimmy's. "I love you too." With their faces only inches away, they held each other's gaze.

"I'm on my knees."

In spite of the ache in his chest, Eli smiled at Jimmy's asinine comment. "I know. Are they hurting yet?"

Jimmy shook his head. Their foreheads squished together at the motion, pulling a chuckle from Eli. "Can I ask you a question?"

Eli didn't hesitate. "Of course."

"What did you spend the three thousand on?"

Eli understood Jimmy's need to change the subject. His chest hurt, but Jimmy was the important one at the moment. Eli could cry later. Now, he'd be the person Jimmy needed. Eli chewed on his bottom lip, biting back a smile before answering, "Hookers and beer."

"Oh my God. You still have it," Jimmy

said, sounding disbelieving.

Eli rushed to reassure him. "No. I spent it. Just ask me something, okay?"

Jimmy's smile returned. "Oooh, a secret. I'll figure this out, you know?"

Heat flooded Eli's cheeks. He hated being put on the spot. Jimmy was on the verge of ruining something special to Eli. "You will find out eventually, but not today, okay?"

Jimmy's smile fell. His expression turned serious. "Okay, since this is obviously important to you, I'll drop it."

"Thank you."

"Will you marry me?"

"Ask me something else."

"No," Jimmy said, denying Eli for the first time ever and proving he knew Eli better than anyone on the planet. "Marry me," Jimmy repeated, refusing to let Eli throw away something they both knew he wanted.

"We've only been together eight months."

Jimmy's face hardened. "And if you think that small detail would stop me from following you to the ends of the Earth, you're in for a shock if you ever decide to leave me."

"Okay."

Jimmy's brow furrowed. "Okay, what?"

"Is that your next question?"

Jimmy tried smacking Eli's ass without luck since he was sitting on it.

Eli chuckled, still wondering if he would hyperventilate even as he agreed to alter their relationship forever. "Okay. Let's get married."

*

Jimmy watched the words leave Eli's gorgeous lips with a sense of disconnect. He hadn't expected the man to agree. His proposal had been one hundred percent genuine, but he'd been prepared to spend the next few months begging—just as he had when he convinced Eli to quit his job. Now, Jimmy didn't know how to react. He'd known all along he wanted this, but his past had been standing in the way. It wasn't fair to tie Eli to his side without knowing. Jace had taken care of that. Eli, proving how wonderful he truly was, wasn't afraid. Even knowing where Jimmy came from, he still wanted to spend the rest of his life with Jimmy.

"Are you being serious?"

Eli nodded. "You told me you'd try harder to ask for what you want. I can't ask for anything more direct than that. I'd be honored to be married to you."

Jimmy was speechless. He'd never dreamed anyone would be honored to do anything at all with him—much less tie themselves to his side for life. "So, you're serious?"

The smile stretching Eli's lips went further to ease Jimmy's mind than anything. "Yes."

"You both have the biggest smiles on your face. I had to come over and join in," Logan said, interrupting before Jimmy could think of anything to say.

He pointed at Eli. "He just agreed to marry me."

Logan blinked. "Seriously?"

"That's what I said," Jimmy said, sounding over-the-top excited even to his ears.

"Oh my God. That's amazing," Logan said, leaning down and pulling off an amazing group hug. Their celebration drew a crowd.

Malik moved in. "What did I miss?"

Logan beamed. "Jimmy asked Eli to marry him, and Eli said yes."

"Really?" Malik said, sounding shocked.

Eli snorted. "Why does everyone seem so surprised?"

At Eli's question, Malik visibly tried to rearrange his features into a smile. "I just never thought I'd see the day when Jimmy got his shit straight."

"Hey," Jimmy said, without any real heat. He knew Malik spoke the truth.

Malik kept talking as if Jimmy hadn't said anything. "But I'm thrilled." Turning his head, Malik released an ear-piercing whistle, bringing the entire club to a halt. All eyes turned their way. "Jimmy asked Eli to marry him. He said yes." Catcalls rent the air. Jimmy couldn't tear his gaze away from Eli. The man's face was blood red and his hand covered his eyes. Normally, Jimmy would try saving the man from being the center of attention. In this case, he wanted everyone to know Eli belonged to him.

Several people surrounded them, offering their congrats, and Jimmy came to his feet. Jimmy noticed Jace wasn't one. The man's expression spoke volumes. It was apparent he didn't think he should join in. Even though they hadn't been meant for each other, Jimmy still felt guilty. He hadn't really tried to be better for Jace. They hadn't even slept together, because Jimmy's body wanted nothing to do with it. He knew he'd made the man feel unwanted, and now he was marrying someone else. Jimmy couldn't blame Jace for staying put. Jace caught him staring. Jimmy dipped his chin, hoping the man understood it was an apology. Jace gave him a jerky nod in return. It would have to be enough.

"What's all this?"

Jimmy's head whipped around at the sound of Tyler's voice. "What are you doing here?"

Tyler waved a hand in Eli's direction. "Eli said you work out here. I thought I'd check out the place." He motioned toward where Sam stood at his back. "This gentleman was giving me a tour when I spotted you. Did you win a big match or something?"

Jimmy noticed Eli wouldn't meet his

gaze. He hadn't known Eli and Tyler had been talking. The man was full of secrets today. "I asked Eli to marry me."

"That's awesome," Tyler said without waiting for the rest. It was obvious he didn't believe Eli would answer with anything other than a yes. "I won't intrude."

"Congratulations," Sam said quietly, but Jimmy couldn't tear his gaze away from Tyler.

"You're not intruding. You're family."

Tyler looked away. His gaze landed on some point over Jimmy's shoulder. "Eli will be one hell of a husband. I'm happy for you." Jimmy didn't understand why Tyler couldn't look at him as he said the words. He let it slide for now. He finally met Jimmy's gaze once more. "I guess you could use that trip to Cooper Island Eli booked for your honeymoon."

Jimmy's jaw slackened. "What?"

"Goddamn it, Tyler. That was a surprise for his birthday," Eli said, looking hurt.

Damn. Tyler was telling on Eli all over the place today. In this case, Jimmy was upset on Eli's behalf. This was obviously important. He stepped around Tyler, ignoring everything else. "You got me a trip to Cooper Island?"

Eli nodded, still looking hurt. "That's what I did with the money."

Now Jimmy understood why Eli had asked him not to push. "If it makes you feel any better, I don't even know where that's at."

A small smile touched Eli's lips, taking away some of the pressure in Jimmy's chest. "It's a secluded island in the Virgin Islands. You asked me once if we could run away. Since it never happened, I thought I'd give you your wish for your birthday."

Those clear green eyes he'd fallen in love with stared at Jimmy now, filled with hope. "I'm sorry Tyler ruined your surprise, but that's amazing. He's right, though. That would be the perfect honeymoon."

Eli licked his lips. The nervous gesture made Jimmy want to kiss him. "Your birthday is only a little more than a month away."

"Is that a problem?"

The world fell away as Jimmy waited for Eli's answer. Never in a million years would Jimmy have dreamed he would fall in love and beg someone to marry him in less than a year's time, but here he was.

Eli shook his head. "It's actually kind of perfect. You said you wanted to run away and keep me all to yourself on a secluded island. So let's do it. Let's elope and spend our honeymoon hidden away. I love the thought of making your dream come true."

"You've already done that," Jimmy said without missing a beat. It was the truth. The day Eli had shown up, money in hand, he'd done more than restore his faith in people. He'd given Jimmy hope. Maybe to the rest of the world, they were unstable and imperfect. To Jimmy, they were beautiful.

Keep an eye out for the next book in the Hooked series, *Unarm*.

Author Bio

Charity Parkerson is an award winning and multi-published author with several companies. Born with no filter from her brain to her mouth, she decided to take this odd quirk and insert it in her characters.

*2015 Readers' Favorite Award Winner
*Winner of 2, 2014 Readers' Favorite Awards
*2015 Passionate Plume Award Finalist
*2013 Readers' Favorite Award Winner
*2013 Reviewers' Choice Award Winner
*2012 ARRA Finalist for Favorite Paranormal Romance
*Five-time winner of The Mistress of the Darkpath

Connect with her online:

--Website: charityparkerson.com
--Facebook:
facebook.com/authorCharityParkerson
facebook.com/TheMenofSin
--Twitter: twitter.com/CharityParkerso